"Definitely." He exhaled, hard. He put his phone on the couch and then dropped his head into his hands, rubbing his temples. "None of this is making any sense—my brother being here, my father making and spending that kind of money, and why they ended up dead."

"We will figure it out." She stood up and walked over to him, then sat down on the couch next to him. She put her hand on his shoulder and leaned closer until their legs touched. It was a simple touch, but warmth radiated between them like shared breath. "But your dad wasn't selling drugs or anything, was he?" she teased with a laugh to lighten the mood.

"The closest thing my dad ever got to drugs was beer—he did like his Banquets." He smiled at what must have been the memory. "In fact, it's fair to say most of the charges at the gas stations were probably for a tank of gas, Copenhagen and a case of beer." He reached up and put his hand on hers.

"Then he was a true Montana rancher." She smiled at him as he stroked the back of her hand with his thumb.

"Did you admit your father is terrible with money?"

RODEO CRIME RING

DANICA WINTERS

INTRIGUE

Thank you to all my readers.

It is an incredible feeling to know our worlds meet, even if it is only for a moment on the page.

Harlequin® INTRIGUE™

ISBN-13: 978-1-335-45748-6

Rodeo Crime Ring

Copyright © 2025 by Danica Winters

 Harlequin Enterprises ULC
22 Adelaide St. West, 41st Floor
Toronto, Ontario M5H 4E3, Canada
www.Harlequin.com

Printed in Lithuania

MIX
Paper | Supporting responsible forestry
FSC® C021394

Danica Winters is a multiple-award-winning, bestselling author who writes books that grip readers with their ability to drive emotion through suspense and occasionally a touch of magic. When she's not working, she can be found in the wilds of Montana, testing her patience while she tries to hone her skills at various crafts—quilting, pottery and painting are not her areas of expertise. She believes the cup is neither half-full nor half-empty, but it better be filled with wine. Visit her website at danicawinters.net.

Visit the Author Profile page at Harlequin.com.

Chapter One

The smell of cows only meant one thing to Cameron Trapper and his Montana family on the West Glacier Cattle Ranch—*money.*

The bigger the stink, the better they'd weathered the winter and the larger the operation could grow. He rolled down the pickup's window and let the wind pour in. This summer, the air smelled too much like roses.

In the distance sat the shiny green bailer. Last summer, his father, Leonard, had taken out another note of credit and purchased the newest model, complete with heat and air-conditioning. It was one heck of a step up from the swather and the tall, log beaverslides Cameron had grown up using on their ranch when his grandparents had been running the place.

His father had never been great with money and, even though beef prices were higher than ever, he'd found a great way to drive the ranch into the ground.

He thought of the old beaverslides. They had been so fun to play with as a kid. His family had used the tractors to move the cut hay to the elevator-style lifts that cranked the hay up the slide and dumped it into large, fenced piles. When they ran out of room in one fence, they'd move the huge slides to the next spot with the tractor and start the process all over again.

It was old tech, and an even older tradition, but it worked better than the new bailer his father had purchased. It used less gas, plus it also kept wildlife like deer and elk from grazing on their family's much-needed winter hay supply for the cattle. Not only had his father cost them the note, but he'd also tripled their gas bill and they'd ended up having to buy hay for their herd last winter.

Cameron was so mad at Leonard that he could almost cuss.

Modernization might be their ruin.

It was a Montana tradition and possibly a tale as old as the state itself—multiple generations of hard work and sacrifice brought down by one bad trustee.

He would put a stop to it, dammit.

His couldn't be like every other family who'd worked hard for their brand—like the P Lazy J and the D◊H— who'd then watched them become nothing more than a decoration hanging on their living room walls.

Yet, Montana was being hit by a land grab like he'd never seen before, perpetuated by deep pockets. The worst part about it was that the ranch was sitting at its epicenter and his father wasn't ready for the war.

When he rolled up to the barn, Leonard was sitting on the ground by the back tire of his pickup, his arms over his chest and his hat tipped low. Cameron didn't understand how his father could have been sleeping on a day like this, one with plenty of work that needed doing.

He pulled his truck next to his father's and made sure to slam the door a little extra hard to jerk him awake. His father didn't stir.

Trying to control his rage, Cameron walked to the barn

and slid open the door, the caster squeaking as loudly as it had since as early as he could remember. Ginger was in her stall and she stuck her head out and nickered as he walked into the damp, musty-smelling barn. They needed to open this place up and get it dried out and ready for hay.

"How's it going, old lady?" he asked the blaze-faced mare. "You gonna play nice or are you feeling a little hot? I saw you looking at that young roan stud yesterday. You better not be getting any ideas." He gave the horse a loving, gentle scratch behind her ear as he chastised.

The bay mare closed her eyes and dropped her head as he rubbed, and they both seemed to acknowledge that her glory days as a brood mare were past. Now, Ginger was devoted to him and the occasional neighborhood kid who came through the barn during baling season.

His father's paint, Bessie, came sidling up to the other stall's door and gave him the side-eye like she could read his feelings toward her rider. "Don't worry, he'll be along. Or do you want me to saddle you up, too?" he asked Bessie as he grabbed the tack for Ginger.

The paint blew snot at him as he walked by her carrying Ginger's saddle.

She was definitely his father's horse.

Ginger was an angel, even exhaling as he tightened the saddle. Bessie, on the other hand, held her breath and puffed up when he tried to tighten the cinch.

"If you don't watch it, you're going to the glue factory." He didn't mean it, but that horse really was something else.

He walked them out of the barn before he stepped into Ginger's saddle and grabbed Bessie's reins. As she moved, the paint let out her breath and the saddle on her back shifted to the left. It couldn't feel good on the mare's back, but his father would have to tighten her up when she got over her attitude.

He rode over toward his resting father. "You getting up, lazy bones?"

There wasn't an answer. His father must have really tied one on last night.

"Hey, old man, you awake?" he called over the crunch of the horses' footfalls on the gravel in the driveway.

Bessie let out a huff and a nicker, throwing her head like she was trying to pull the reins out of his hands and head back to the barn. Instead of letting her, he held on tighter and gave them a little nudge. Bessie stopped and refused to budge, leaning back into her haunches.

"Are you freaking kidding me? You old pain in the..." He gave the reins another pull to get her moving, but she leaned back even farther. She turned her head and the whites of her eyes were showing—he didn't know why, or of what, but Bessie was afraid.

He dropped her reins and before they even touched the ground, she spun on her back hooves and raced toward the barn. She disappeared into the barn and away from them. Ginger looked back at him like she was hoping he would lead her away as well, but had a cool enough head to wait and not get into an impromptu rodeo.

She would be getting an extra flake of hay tonight.

He nudged Ginger forward. His father could deal with Bessie in a minute. First, he needed to figure out what was bothering the animals.

His thoughts moved to his father's note. They couldn't handle any more predation or losses on the ranch. Not if they wanted to be in the black.

Ginger took a tentative step toward the pickups, to where his father had been sitting.

"Dad?" he asked once more.

Again, no answer. Maybe he had run inside or something while Cameron had been saddling up the horses.

Ginger moved forward, but only thanks to his goading her with the press of his thighs. She drew in a long breath and exhaled hard, nickering. She didn't like her task, but she plodded forward, dragging her hooves.

As he neared Leonard's pickup, where Cameron had last seen his father resting, Ginger snorted and threw her head. "Whoa, girl. It's okay," he cooed, trying to calm his spooked mare.

She took another step but then stopped and refused to be urged another. Horses were smart—smarter than cows and definitely smarter than most people. If Ginger was spooked, something was very wrong.

He gave her a pat on the side of her neck and she looked back at him, concern in her eyes, as though she was trying to tell him what he was clearly too stupid to already know.

The last time he'd seen her act like this they had edged up on a rattlesnake in the Red Rocks. The way she was acting now—there was something deadly and darned close.

A griz had been skulking around the ranch the last month or so, but it hadn't posed a real threat. Hopefully, the bear hadn't decided to start causing problems. The last thing they needed was the game wardens coming out and poking around.

That was to say nothing about the wolves who had gotten to five of their calves this spring. Even though they had insurance on the cattle and their losses of the calves had been a stipend, it didn't cover the real losses of possible sales prices—at least with the price of beef being what it was.

He backed his horse up and turned her away from the

truck. As he had her move, she seemed to relax under him. Whatever was wrong was by that truck and near where his father had been.

He stepped down out of the saddle and looped the reins over the edge of the truck's tailgate. Ginger wouldn't take them and run; for her, the idea of being tied up was enough for her to stay put. Unless things went totally haywire.

Though he considered calling out to his father one more time, Cameron stopped himself. If his father was still out here, he would be in no shape to answer, or he would have spoken up already. He steeled himself as he walked around the pickup. Leonard's boots came into view in exactly the same position he'd seen them when he'd first arrived.

The world dissolved around him as he stared at the tip of those boots. They were so dirty and caked with muck that they were nearly black except in the places where the muck had dried and turned gray. A piece of hay stuck out from his heel. For a long moment, Cameron just stared at the piece of grass. It was faded green and moldy, folded in the middle, like his father had just happened to pick it up on his heel while he'd gone around his morning chores.

It was so *normal*, but he couldn't help fixating on the little thing as he comprehended the reasons why his father wouldn't have been answering—or moving.

He pushed forward, goading himself like he had his mare. She had been right; things were fifty shades of wrong.

His father's face was partially hidden by his black cowboy hat, but now that he was closer and not just rolling by, Cameron could see that his father's skin was an eerie shade of gray—the same color of that dead calf's lips and tongue, the tint of bloodlessness.

There was a silver-and-elk-antler hilt sticking out from

under his father's folded arms, which looked like they were resting on the object. His dad had carried a Ruana knife just like that one on his belt every day of his life—except when he'd put on his Sunday clothes for churchgoing.

Cameron squatted down beside his father and put his finger to his leathery neck, though he knew exactly what he'd fail to find.

Part of him half expected his father to sit up and exclaim some stupid thing like this was some sick joke, but he remained still and his arms stayed folded over his chest, resting on that damned knife.

Without thinking, Cameron took out his phone and dialed 9-1-1. While he talked, he started taking pictures of his father's body and the area around him.

Questions raced through his mind about what had happened to the family's controversial patriarch and how. But one thing was certain—his father was gone.

The crown he'd left behind would be almost as heavy as the family's loss.

Chapter Two

If Emily Monahan had known the Glock 19 she'd bought at the ranch supply store would be the gun someone would try to murder her with, she would have never made the purchase. The one thing Emily Monahan didn't have was the knowledge of what the future would bring

She tapped at the gun tightly wrapped in the bellyband around her center mass. The handgun was a little too big to be totally concealed, even though she and her chest were larger than the average woman, and the end of the magazine could be seen if she breathed just a little too hard.

Truth be told, she liked the fact that if someone was really paying attention, they would know she was carrying a concealed weapon in addition to her service weapon. It was the people who would notice who were truly her enemies or her allies.

She definitely had plenty of enemies—in the small town of West Glacier, just outside Glacier National Park, people could be incredibly kind or brutally cruel. As a sheriff's deputy for six years running, she had seen more than her fair share of the latter.

She stared out at the courthouse as she prepped her squad car for the day and took a sip of her coffee. The white building stood in stark contrast to the snowcapped mountains in the background.

As of late, cruelty wasn't just something she was facing at work. Her divorce from Todd had been the stuff of nightmares—mostly thanks to the shared parenting plan they were trying to renegotiate. Though they had been divorced for two years, Todd was now contesting the parenting plan and was demanding they revise.

At the beginning of her exit from their marriage, she'd promised herself their daughter, Stacy, wouldn't be put in the middle. Yet, no matter how hard she'd tried to keep her five-year-old safe and out of lawyer's offices, they would have their third meeting with the mediator this week.

A sickening lump formed in her stomach at the thought.

Until recently, Emily had never really wanted to commit a crime, but she'd be lying if she said she hadn't considered taking her daughter and making a run for the Canadian border. If they just ran, this nightmare could come to an end.

Todd Monahan hadn't been a bad man when they'd met. He'd seemed pretty good, actually. He'd opened the car doors, said all the right things; he'd been working a stable job as a pharmacy technician. On their first date, he'd shown up with flowers not only for her but for her mom, who had been alive and staying with her at the time. Her mother, Julie Moore, had taken an instant liking to him.

Before the wedding, Emily could still recall the moment over the bathroom sink, in her wedding dress, when she was trying to catch her breath between sobs. Her mother had put her hand on the center of her back, her touch cool against Emily's sweating skin. She'd told her mother she wasn't ready, that she couldn't make the walk down the aisle, but her mom had told her that those kinds of nerves were normal and *to be expected on a girl's wedding day*.

Thinking back, the fact that her mother had called it a *girl's* wedding day should have been one of many clues that she had been far too young and not nearly experienced enough to understand the choice she had been making.

To this day, she wasn't sure she knew what true love was—except when it came to her daughter. She'd do anything for that little blond nugget. She smiled as she recalled this morning's tiff over whether Stacy would wear the pink Minnie Mouse bow in her hair or the red Mickey one. In the end, Emily had given up and let her wear both. She couldn't really blame her. At five years old, no colors clashed—there was only what she loved with a dash of something else she adored—and damn if it didn't end up looking completely adorable.

Maternal love was chemical and, for many women, undeniable. It was as natural as the rain and just as critical for a child's healthy development.

The kind of true love she couldn't understand, or believe in, was the kind that came from a partner. When she'd initially been with Todd, she'd thought she'd known what love was—at the time, she'd assumed it was promises of a shared future and fidelity. It was dreams of rings, houses, children and everything down to a little white dog. It was a future of easy choices, *shared choices*, which would be rationally discussed and agreed upon. Then their lives would be beautiful, all the way to their perfectly matching dinner plates and immaculate lawn.

Now she knew that when love was easy and beautiful… that wasn't the true love she had envisioned. With Todd, "easy and beautiful" had meant he had been staying silent to keep the peace and seeking the gritty challenge that came with another woman.

True love in a partnership was a lie.

By the time she'd found out about the other woman, or rather *women*, her mother had passed away from breast cancer. It was stupid, but there were nights when she wanted to rage against her mother's ghost and tell her how wrong she had been to try to mollify her daughter over that sink on the day of her wedding. In fact, her mother would have been better off putting Emily's face in the water, rinsing off the paint that masked the features of the young girl, and helping her to run away.

Emily would never put her own daughter in a situation where she felt forced.

Then again, she had told herself she would never put her daughter in the middle of the fight with Todd—and look where that had gotten her.

Never was Fate's call to arms. Maybe, just maybe, one of these days, she would figure out a way to say never and actually be able to keep the promise.

She instinctively touched her ring finger with her thumb, looking for the band that had reminded her far too much of a handcuff. There was an indent in her skin where it had been up until the day Todd's lawyer had asked to have it returned.

She'd thrown it on the floor at the attorney's feet. If Todd and his team were to be so petty, then she had been fine with them hitting their knees to pick it up.

She cringed at the thought of attorneys. By and large, she would be fine with every last one of them enduring a slow death.

And that was to say nothing of the defense attorneys she ran into on a regular basis in the office. Some of those lawyers were slicker than an oiled-up serpent and far less likable.

Coffee…she just needed coffee and to remember to take one moment and one day at a time. She was in control of her life and her emotions. The second she allowed anyone else to dictate her feelings was when she'd start losing what mattered to her the most.

Emily glanced down at Stacy's picture that was stuck in the corner of her dashboard. Her daughter was smiling up from the paper, one of her front teeth was missing and she was holding a dollar bill like it was some kind of prized fish.

The call log on her computer screen moved as another call popped up, requiring her attention. According to the dispatcher, there was a report of an unwitnessed death on the WGC Ranch. The dispatcher noted that the man was seventy-six years old but, aside from that, there wasn't any more information about the decedent.

As she was the acting coroner for the Flathead County Sheriff's Office, it fell upon Emily to handle this situation. Being the coroner on call gave her a leg up at the office, allowing her to gain more Peace Officer Standard and Training or POST Certifications, but it did little for her social life. Few of her friends really wanted to talk about dead bodies, not really. Sure, they had a morbid curiosity, like many, and they could handle hearing about the latest death or interesting case, but when it came right down to it, she wasn't about to tell them the truth about what she saw out there while working.

No one wanted to know what pets did to a human body after a person died. It was safe to say that while she liked them, she was not going to be owning a cat any time in the near future. She had simply seen too much.

She let the dispatcher know she was en route to West Glacier Cattle Ranch and then flipped on the radio and listened to the latest country music. Though Dispatch had posted the address, it was unnecessary; she drove by their front gate more often than she cared to admit during her days on patrol. The ranch sat just off Highway 2 East and was tucked into one of the languid bellies of the glacial moraines of the Lewis Mountains.

It was the location that, she had to assume, kept the Trapper family ranching. By and large, most of the rest of their sleepy little town was being swept up in the scurry for land deals by out-of-staters who wanted to make the picturesque town into their personal playground. It was rare these days to see any parcels larger than a handful of acres. Taxes were getting too high for a working ranch to survive, even with the agricultural breaks—or so she'd read in the *Daily Interlake* and heard from the few old timers who were left and still frequented the out-of-the-way diner, the Coffee Cup.

The diner had been around even longer than Emily and she had grown up drinking out of the heavy brown mugs that she was sure the owners had bought sometime in the 1970s. Once in a while, when she went there in the early morning hours, she would still spot one of the mugs float by on a waitress's tray, but these days, most of them had been replaced by the cheaper white ones. Seeing those chipped and fading brown mugs saddened her though she really couldn't explain why.

The entrance to the ranch was coming up, complete with the log archway decorated with the company's hanging iron brand. As she turned, the brand listed in the wind and, as it moved, she spotted a smattering of rust eating away at its black surface.

She had grown up in Kalispell, the biggest city nearest to the little town, but besides playing sports and a couple of dates with a receiver from the area, she hadn't known many of the people who had lived in West Glacier—at least not when she'd been growing up. Now, she had a few places that she frequently visited, thanks to either tumultuous romantic partners, family feuds, or criminal behaviors, but most callouts to the area were for minor things.

People usually kept to themselves, and when she did have to make traffic stops, she was usually treated with kindness and deference. Though there were outliers to every generalization.

As Emily slowed down and turned onto the road that led into the ranch, she spotted two saddled horses munching on grass on the inside of the cattle guard that sat across the end of the driveway. The bay looked up at her and swished its tail, almost as if waving hello, but the paint turned its back as she approached, and she noted that its saddle was sitting lopsided. The cattle guard sat across the end of the driveway, keeping them from getting hit by highway traffic but little more.

She liked horses, but since they were so far from the barn, untied, and not being used, it told her that they had probably been at the epicenter of some major drama. No cowboy worth his Wranglers would ever leave a horse out like those two. If left too long, the paint would get sores from that saddle, and that was the least of their worries if they decided to take a jump over the guard.

She was tempted to stop the car, grab the horses and lead them back to the barn, but this wasn't her ranch, and maybe these horses had been out there for some reason. She needed to take care of business first and then she could come back for them.

Then again, if that paint had been carrying that lop-sided saddle for a while, it might have been hurting. She hated seeing animals in pain. Besides, she was out here to pick up a body and if she didn't get there in five minutes, it wasn't like they could get *more* dead.

She pulled her car over to the side of the driveway and stepped out. "Hello, babies," she called in a singsong voice.

The bay started to walk toward her, slowly, as if trying to decide whether or not she was to be trusted. The paint didn't even acknowledge her and instead continued to graze on the green grass and move in the opposite direction.

She walked toward the more amiable horse and took hold of its reins, gently scratching it behind the ear. The mare had a beautiful saddle, its leather worn and darkened with time and age, but it had been oiled and well maintained over the years.

"You're a beautiful girl," she said, leading the horse to the white fence. She looped the rein around the top slat. "You go ahead and wait here, babe, and I'm gonna go and try to get your comrade over there all fixed up. Okay?" She gave the mare a gentle pat and made her way toward the paint.

The paint took a step away from her, swishing her tail and pinning her ears back in Emily's direction. "Hey, beautiful," she cooed, trying to move slowly so as not to spook the horse.

The horse huffed.

"Yes, you know I want to take care of you," she said, trying to keep her voice soft but authoritative. She stepped around the paint and took hold of the horse's reins. The paint tried to throw her head, but Emily applied a slight bit of pressure and checked the horse. This one didn't need to think it was in control.

She stepped toward the fence. The horse didn't want to move her feet at first, but Emily wouldn't take no for an answer and, finally, the horse took a couple of tentative steps in the right direction. "Good, girl, we've got this," she said, trying to reinforce the desired behavior.

There had been many days like this on her grandparents' ranch on the east side of the state. They'd had a five-thousand-acre ranch on the outskirts of Havre and near the Rocky Boy Reservation. Every spring she would come up and help round up the cattle for cutting and branding. She hadn't been there in the last ten years, ever since her eldest brother had taken over the ranch. She missed it, but she wasn't about to work with her brother. That man had a mean streak a mile wide and a mouth dirtier than any sailor she had ever met.

She would never understand why her grandfather had chosen her brother to inherit the place. Then again, her brother was one of the hardest workers she had ever met. There was nothing that man couldn't fix and no cow that could slip his rope. It just gnawed at her that as the younger and female member of the family, she hadn't been considered to take over the family's business.

In all reality, she couldn't complain about where life had taken her. She loved her work in law enforcement. Besides, if she had taken over the ranch, it would have been expected that she would have had to get married and let her husband take the helm—at least, according to the unspoken generational rules handed down by her German great-grandparents, who had come to this country in hopes of changing their and their children's futures. In some ways, the only thing they had done was change their familial location. Many of the toxic behaviors had come right along with them and had been passed down.

Everything had been conditional on her playing by the rules. She had never been very good at being told what she could or could not do; as such, maybe it wasn't such a mystery as to why her brother had been selected to control the family's legacy.

The paint nickered and blew out a little bubble of snot. "You feel okay, pumpkin?" she asked, wrapping the rein around the fence before stepping back and readjusting the saddle. The horse exhaled hard, letting her pull the cinch tight. "There you go, that ought to feel better." She pulled the leather rein free of the fence and climbed up into the saddle.

She nudged the paint in the direction of the bay and, taking the rein off the fence, she led the bay back toward the ranch. The house was at least a mile away from the road and where she had parked her squad car. When they came into view of the barn, the paint started to speed up. The horse made her smile; it had one heck of a personality. She wasn't a horse that would be good for someone who didn't have a ton of experience in handling.

For so many reasons, the beautiful horse made her miss having her own.

The barn was bright red with white trim, and it looked as though it had been painted in the last year or two. The family must have been doing well, or they were up to their eyeballs in debt. She hoped it wasn't the latter. Ranching was a fickle business, and everything could change in the blink of an eye or a springtime hard freeze.

Her brother had told her he had been forced to sell off most of his cattle last year because of a dry summer, which had led to an even drier fall. Every crop that had managed to make it through the hard scrabble had then been gobbled up by hordes of grasshoppers. According to Josh, they had only managed to make pennies on the dollar—and that was before they'd had to pay the cutters.

There was a collection of dented-up pickups, all of which were covered in mud and bits of grass. A couple of the trucks that were parked nearest to the barn were so old that she wondered if they were even capable of turning over or if they had become lawn ornaments. A man with a white cowboy hat and a red-flannel shirt had his back turned to her as she approached with the horses. There was the distinctive Copenhagen can mark in the back pocket of his jeans, the wear mark that was as much a part of cowboy culture as beer and buckles.

The horses' hoofs crunched on the gravel and the man turned. Even under the brim of his hat, she could tell he had blue eyes that were almost the same tone as the sunny sky. His hair poked out from under the band, making a swoop at the nape of his neck. It was a little long, but he was the kind of cowboy that could make any hairstyle look good.

His chin had a patch of dirt where he must have rubbed the back of his fist against his scruff. In his hand was a cell phone and he had it pressed against his ear. He was a strange juxtaposition between the old ways and the new, but something about him and the way he looked made her want to know more about the mystery of him.

"I gotta go," he said, his voice was as gravely as the driveway. He clicked off the phone and gave her an acknowledging tip of the hat as she slipped out of the saddle. "Glad you could make it." He looked at his watch. "I called you guys over an hour ago."

She wasn't sure what to make of his icy greeting. Sure,

the guy was having one heck of a day, but that still didn't mean he had to be less than civil. "It took me a little longer than expected. I found these two roaming close to the highway," she said, playing nice in an attempt to give the man the benefit of the doubt about whether or not his attitude was situational or habitual. "This one here," she said, motioning to the paint, "nearly had her saddle upside down."

He sighed, running his hand over his face. "Thanks for grabbing the runaways. Last time I checked on them, they had wandered around the back of the barn, so I don't know how they got out there. I thought they were all right. I appreciate you looking out for them." He walked over and took the reins of the bay from her, their fingers grazing against one another, and the simple action caught her so off guard that her breath hitched in her throat.

What was wrong with her? Since when did a man inadvertently brushing against her on a death scene cause this kind of reaction?

She was distracted by that little can mark in his jeans as he walked the horses to the barn and disappeared inside. His momentary absence was welcome; it gave her a moment to come to her senses and remember exactly why she was there.

Brushing her hands over her hair, she tucked a wayward piece behind her ear as she took a look around. In the distance, she could make out the siren of an ambulance.

There were the sounds of footfalls behind her. "Do you want me to take you to him?" Cameron asked.

She nodded, not daring to look back at the man out of the fear he would see the confusing mix of feelings displayed on her face.

Following him, he led her through the mix of trucks to an older model Ford with mud caked over most of its body and wheels. "I found my father like this," he said, motioning toward the back tire.

As she stepped around, an older man came into view. He looked like he was taking a nap—except for the antler-handled knife protruding from his chest. When Dispatch had called, they had told her it was merely an unwitnessed death. She had been led to believe the man had likely died of natural causes and this was little more than a body retrieval. But what she was looking at was far from a natural death: what she was looking at was murder.

Chapter Three

Cameron couldn't believe how quickly two other cops had shown up at the ranch. Sitting inside a squad car was a deputy who looked to be no more than in his early twenties, with dark hair that was a little too long and a patchy clump of chin hair. Standing near his father's body was a heavy-set detective who looked like he had a baton taped to his spine, or maybe placed somewhere else.

He glanced toward Deputy Monahan, or as he'd heard the older Detective Bullock call her, Emily.

She was standing by the detective and staring at him, and as Cameron caught her looking, he expected her to turn away, but instead they locked eyes for a long awkward moment. She had been looking at him weirdly ever since she had arrived. She must have thought he'd had something to do with his father's death, though that couldn't have been further from the truth.

Sure, he and Leonard had had their fair share of friction and fights, but that didn't mean he'd wanted the man dead. If anything, he would have just wanted his father to retire and get out of the way so the ranch could stand a chance to make it in a world that seemed hell-bent on turning it into a strip mall.

Deputy Monahan said something to Bullock and walked

over toward him. She had her thumb jammed under her utility belt and her palm resting on the grip of her pistol. Something in the way she stood made him wonder if she was uncomfortable either with the belt, with the gun or with him. Her brows furrowed as she glanced up at him. "You okay?"

He nodded. "Just thinking about all the chores that need to be done. We were planning on moving the other half of our cattle out of the spring pasture and up onto the range." He pointed toward the mountains behind their ranch where they always let the cattle freely roam during the summer months.

"Will they be okay for another day? You have enough feed?" she asked.

"Another day won't break us, but I was hoping to get them out of the spring grounds so we can get it ready for them to come back in the fall. The less we have to hay, the better."

"I understand." She rested her other hand on her utility belt and he couldn't help but notice the roundness of her hips.

She had the silhouette of his perfect type of woman. Not a woman who was out running marathons for fun maybe, rather one he could hold in his arms and take comfort in her softness. All he really cared about, though, was finding a woman who understood what it took to be with a rancher and love him for who he was.

His ex had told him that she'd understood the long hours and the crazy responsibilities from cleaning stalls and pulling calves to tuning up carburetors. Yet that had proven to be nothing more than pretty old promises pitted against an ugly modern reality. Now, not only was there the coming and goings of ranching, but there was also the paperwork.

The modern farmer and rancher had to have someone on their team who knew how to apply for government grants and programs to help ensure that when times were lean, they were covered against financial ruin. His ex wasn't the first woman who had come to learn what it meant to be a rancher's wife and then hit the road.

"Yeah, thanks." He sighed as he considered the state of the place and what had just fallen on his plate. He almost felt guilty for thinking about the business at a time like this and that even earlier that day he had *wished* to get control. This hadn't been how he'd wanted to gain power. He'd only wanted his father to retire.

"Were you working with your father full-time?" she asked.

He nodded. "I was his right-hand man. Well…I was his primary hand anyway."

She studied him as though she was trying to translate what he'd said. "You guys close?"

He shrugged. "I don't know how many ranching families you know, but if you've been around a few, I'm sure you know that closeness can be a curse as much as it can be a boon. Every little thing can get under your skin."

"That doesn't really answer my question. Or are you telling me you didn't get along?" she countered.

"That's not it," he said, waving her off. "We had our knock-down-drag-outs, but at the end of the day, if either of us needed anything, we knew who we could rely on."

"Any knockdowns lately?"

He didn't like where she was taking these questions. "Look, my father and I butted heads, but I didn't want him dead and, like I've told the detectives, I didn't have anything to do with his death. I found my father out here perched like this. And no, I don't know anyone else who would have wanted him dead, either."

"Have you talked to your mom and told her about your father? Is she around?" she asked.

He shook his head. "She passed away a few years ago. Cancer. She is buried in Sunset Memorial." He motioned toward town.

Deputy Monahan pinched her lips. "I'm sorry to hear that." She paused. "What about siblings?"

He knew she was doing her job, but he was so tired of answering all these questions. "I have a brother who lives out of state. Last I heard, he was rough-necking in North Dakota, but who knows if he is still there. I haven't heard from him in the last year. I also have a sister who is in the wind. She was in Burbank, doing something in Hollywood. And there's my other sister on the rodeo circuit, a barrel racer. Once they left, none looked back." He tried to check the anger and resentment caused by their abandonment from flecking his voice.

He couldn't be angry at the fact that they had seized their chances to get out and away from the prison this ranch had become.

She looked at him, but he didn't want to let her meet his gaze out of some weird feeling that if she did, she would be able to see right through him and she would know all the things he was thinking and feeling. No one needed to know how he felt—feelings were for the weak and in this world only the strongest survived.

"Anyone else work on the ranch, or is it just you and your father?"

He noticed one of the deputies had made his way over and was listening to their conversation even though he wasn't facing him. Cameron was tempted to just tell the guy to turn around and join the conversation, but one questioning him was enough.

"We have managed to keep on a skeleton crew." As he said the word *skeleton* he cringed. "I mean, we have me, my dad and a hand named Trevor, whose been living out at the bunkhouse for the past year, but he's worked at the ranch since he was eighteen. Soon, though, we will hire some kids to come in and buck bales and move irrigation for us." He pulled out his phone and texted his best friend and hand, Trevor Band. "I texted my main guy, but he said he had his kid this morning."

"*Had* his kid?" she asked.

"Yeah, he and his ex-wife share custody." There was a pain in her expression as he mentioned custody, making him wonder if she had her own battle there.

"Do you think he might have seen or talked to your father?"

He shrugged. "I doubt it, but talk to him."

He didn't mean to come off curt, but he didn't know any more than they did about it.

"Do you have anyone else living on the ranch besides you guys?"

He nodded. "Not right now, but soon maybe we will. Like I said, teenagers and cowboys rounding up cows and bucking bales. Low-budget jobs that no one else wants to do and no one sticks around after they've done them."

She pointed at the main house. It stood in stark contrast to the freshly painted barn. The house was the kind that had probably been extraordinary when it had been built in the early 1900s, but now looked as dilapidated as the Sears catalog the model had probably been bought from with its sagging roof and half-missing gables. "Just you and your father live in there?"

He shook his head. "I live in my own house, just down the road." He pointed north.

In Montana speak, *just down the road* could have meant anything from two houses down to two hundred acres away. Time and space didn't really exist in this state; they were more suggestions and reminders.

"Have you been in your father's house recently?" she asked, an air of judgment to her question.

Did she think he was some kind of delinquent son for not wanting to live with his aged father? Was he the bad guy for wanting his own place and some sense of independence from the chaos that was his father?

He instantly felt horrible for his thoughts—he couldn't think badly of his father, not when he was sitting there not a dozen yards from him, dead as a doornail.

Gah. Cameron nearly made the sound aloud. *I'm a monster.* He ran his hand over the back of his neck as he chastised himself for his callousness about his father's demise.

No matter how he had been feeling about the man, he was always his father—dead or alive.

"I haven't," he said. "He didn't keep it locked though. Do you want to take a look around? I'm sure my father wouldn't have minded." He strode past her as he made his way to the front door of the house and he could make out the sound of her footfalls in the gravel as she followed behind.

He heard her say something to the detective, but the wailing of the ambulance on the highway as it passed by drowned out her exact words.

As the sound grew faint and the ambulance moved farther into the distance, somehow their departure saddened him—maybe if he had noticed his father earlier, he would have had a chance to save him. Instead, he'd been so focused on the task at hand and the work that had to be done that he had failed to notice the gravity of the situation.

He was complicit in his father's passing.

Guilt rattled through him, striking every rib and settling deep in his heart, right next to the grief he still held for losing his mother.

No matter what anyone said, some pains never went away—instead, they only waited to be compounded and refreshed.

The front door of the house swung open and he was hit with the metallic scent of blood.

"Hello?" he called out, trying to make sense of the smell when his father lay outside.

"Stop," Emily ordered, unholstering her weapon. "Hey, Sergeant Bullock, we've got something going on in here!" she called to the detective.

The detective rushed over, waving at the kid in the squad car to take over custody of the scene outside. "What's going on, Deputy?"

Emily pulled in a breath. "Do you smell that?" She gave the man a knowing look.

Over the years, they had lost a number of cows to natural causes and disease. The scent of death was unmistakable.

Oddly enough, he hadn't smelled it outside on his father, but standing here inside the doorway of his father's house, it hit him like a mallet.

Death was waiting for them.

"Stay here, Mr. Trapper," the detective said, taking out his gun. He motioned for Emily to follow him.

As the door swung open, Cameron stared down the hallway that led into the main room. There was a long, bloody streak and a handprint near the doorway that led toward the bedrooms. From the direction, it appeared as though someone had walked in and struggled down the hallway.

Had it been his father's killer?

Had his father put up a fight and hurt the person who had killed him?

He felt some comfort in the idea that his father's murderer had been injured and that they possibly lay dead somewhere in the house.

As the two officers made their way inside, cleared the hallway and moved toward the main room, they stopped. Emily said something to the detective Cameron couldn't quite make out.

Cameron wanted to follow them, to go in and find out exactly what had happened and who had played a role in his father's death. He had to know. He had to know who had wished to destroy his family and the ranch. However, he did as the detective had ordered and he stayed outside. In order to see inside, he rushed to the right and the big bay window that looked into the main room. He pressed his face against the glass. Emily was bending down over a man's body. There, lying dead in his family's living room—where he had spent dozens of Christmases opening presents and celebrated a hundred different birthdays—was his rough-necking brother, Ben. His lifeless eyes caught his and, for a long moment, Cameron couldn't look away from the azure that had started to cloud with death.

Those eyes… The last time he had been looking in them, his brother had been telling him he was leaving the ranch and never coming back. Ben had never wanted to step foot back here. He'd never wanted to speak to his father again. Now, both were dead.

Cameron was the last man left alive in his family.

His thoughts swirled, but one rose to the top… No matter how hard he tried, he couldn't understand why his world was suddenly filled with the ghosts of his past—ghosts that would now undoubtedly come to haunt his future.

Chapter Four

Emily stood up after confirming that the man at her feet was, in fact, devoid of a pulse. There was a loud rap on the front window of the ranch house. The sound made her jump, but she tried to cover up her surprise by calmly wiping her fingers on the leg of her pants as she turned in the direction of the jarring sound.

She was met with Cameron's wide eyes and his hands pressing against the glass. His fingertips were almost as white as his face. He was saying something but his voice was muffled and she couldn't make sense of his words.

For some strange and almost primal reason, the fear and pain in his expression made her want to rush to him, but she held back. She had a job to do. Now wasn't the time to give in to any baser instincts and fall for some unnecessary pull from unspoken places in her belly.

Detective Bullock huffed as he looked at her. "Why don't you go talk to your buddy out there? See if you can get an ID on our vic, here."

She nodded as she tried to keep her footsteps at a normal speed as she exited the ranch house's living room and made her way outside.

Cameron hurried toward her as soon as she stepped outside and he put his hand on her arm. "That's my brother. Ben. That's Ben." His words came out in a single breath.

She put her hand on his. "This is your brother?" she repeated, hoping to see something in his face to give her a sense of their relationship, but she was only met with shock.

He nodded.

The human part of her wanted to ask the handsome, shaken cowboy if he was okay, but the law enforcement officer part of her brain held her back. This was an active crime scene and Cameron was now at its epicenter.

His hand tightened on her arm slightly and she caught his gaze. "He…he hasn't been here in years. This doesn't make sense."

She wanted to ask him questions, but she didn't want to step on Detective Bullock's toes.

Inside the house, through the window, Bullock was taking pictures of the scene and tapping away at his phone. He seemed to have relaxed with her outside the room, evidenced by his belly now pressing hard against his shirt, testing the tensile strength of his buttons.

Detective Bullock had never been the type of man who swayed from protocol, and he wouldn't want her doing so, either. In fact, he was so linear and composed that even his gig line was always rigidly straight. To see him waver from perfection and relax when he thought no one was watching made a smile creep over her lips. It brought her some hope that he was at least a little bit human.

As it was, she wasn't sure she would ever come close to measuring up to this man who had a career record that was so long and distinguished that she was surprised it wasn't chiseled in stone outside the courthouse where the sheriff's office was located.

Something about the simple moment helped Emily find her courage. If Bullock found fault in something she did or didn't do, she would ask for forgiveness later. Though she had come to this scene as a coroner, she was still first and foremost a deputy for Flathead County. She could take a statement just as well as anyone else on this scene. She had been the first one here; she had the right. If nothing else, it was better to act now than to get armchair quarter-backed later and called inept or incompetent.

As the only female deputy in their office, she was constantly scrutinized more than anyone else. Sometimes that was okay because, if someone was to let her off without such analysis, there would have been another person in the office who would be only too happy to wonder if there was something untoward happening between them in the bedroom.

It may have been a modern world, but sexism was still alive and well in this little corner of the world—and it wasn't being aimed at her by just the men in the office but also by the female staff members.

The only thing she could do was what she did best, push her chin up and ignore the chatter. If someone didn't have direct control over her life, then they had no right to levy their opinions onto her psyche.

Though she was good at putting up a brave front, she was insecure enough on her own without stopping to add the weight of what everyone else thought.

She turned to Cameron and readjusted her utility belt slightly. As she moved, the Glock in her bellyband pressed hard against the front of her shirt and she noticed his gaze flicker down to the gun.

"Cam," she started, truncating his name in an effort to instantly gain some bonding ground, "why don't you and

I step over to the barn?" She tapped his hand on her arm, motioning him to release.

As though he hadn't noticed his hand upon her, he let go. He opened his mouth, like he was about to start apologizing, but then stopped himself. "Yes." He turned from her, walking onto the gravel driveway and toward the barn.

Deputy Vetter gave him a tip of the head as Cameron walked past the young officer's car. Vetter would be there until Detective Bullock released the scene or another deputy came along to relieve him in the chain of custody. She waved at him to follow just in case she needed him to stay with their man here.

"Cam, can you tell me a little bit about your family?" He looked at her for a long minute as though, for the first time, he was seeing her as his enemy. She didn't like the feeling. "Don't worry," she added, trying to make his expression disappear. "I just have to ask you a few questions for the detective. He will want to know more about your brother, I'm sure."

He seemed to relax, but it didn't really assuage the feeling in her stomach, which made her feel a bit like a fox in the henhouse.

"He is an oil worker out of North Dakota. Thirty." He rattled off his birthday. "He hasn't been married, but he always seem to have women around him."

"Do you know of anyone who he would have considered an enemy?"

He thought about the question for a long moment before shaking his head. "He and I weren't close enough for me to know something like that. To be honest, you would probably be better off going to social media to find anything out about his private life."

She nodded. "I have a sister like that, I completely understand. She and I never speak, not after my divorce."

His eyebrows shot up and, as soon as they did, she wished she could have reeled in her statement. This man wasn't her friend, she didn't know why she had said anything personal to him. He had no business knowing anything about her—it had been inappropriate of her to speak as she had. Why couldn't she seem to remember who she was around this man?

The last thing he needed to know was that she was damaged.

Never mind that thought. Just because she was divorced and had a history didn't mean she was damaged; it could have just meant she had boundaries—what did he know? She adjusted her utility belt and dabbed slightly at the tip of her nose as she tried to reaffirm her composure.

Thankfully, Deputy Vetter came to her rescue. "How can I help you, Monahan?"

"Would you mind standing here with our friend for a minute?" She put her hand on Cameron's shoulder, like he was her friend—one she was trying to keep just close enough to remain communicating but far enough to keep the strange pull at her core from becoming too strong.

Vetter nodded. "Sure, no problem."

Cameron exhaled as she dropped her hand from his arm, but she tried not to read anything into the sound as it could have meant nearly anything.

Before her thoughts could run away, she smiled. "I'll be right back. I just want to talk to Bullock." She hurried to the house, knowing she could have merely texted him the vic's identity instead of telling him about the information in person.

Whatever, though, it wouldn't hurt for Bullock to see her.

Making her way inside, she was hit with the coppery scent of blood once again. It made her wonder how long it would stay in the house before it would turn into one of fetid death.

Emily tapped on the doorjamb to get Bullock's attention. He sucked in his stomach as she entered the living room. He ran his hand over waxed hair, smoothing what was already perfected. Like he noticed her watching him from outside the front door of the house, he motioned to her with a flick of his finger. She hated that he beckoned her and that she answered like a well-trained pup, but in her job, he was her master—there was no getting around their hierarchy.

"Detective?" she asked, coming to a stop before him.

He peered down his nose at her, the tip was so large that she wondered how he could even fully see her. "Did you get a name?"

She nodded. "It is the son of the man outside. A man name Ben Trapper."

Bullock frowned. "Any idea what the relationship was between father and son? I'm assuming Cameron is his brother?"

She nodded. "Ben was estranged from the family, from the sounds of things. I didn't have time for much more."

"That's okay. Thanks for the start."

She was surprised the detective was satisfied. He wasn't usually the kind to accept the minimum.

She looked inside the living room where the man was lying on the floor. There was a pool of blood around his head, drawing her attention to the hole in the side of his temple. There was a Glock21 in his right hand, his finger still trapped in the trigger guard. "Is there something I can help you with in your investigation?"

Bullock knelt down beside the body on the floor and

stared at the man's hand holding the gun. There was something about the angle of the victim's fingers that drew her
attention. His pointer finger was stiffening in a curl, but
the finger was well over the trigger—almost so far that
it would have made it challenging for him to have pulled
effectively.

"What do you notice about this man?" Bullock asked,
motioning to the decedent's remains.

Ben Trapper's face was longer than his brother's, but
they both had the same chiseled jawline. Ben had a thick
wad of hair on his chin in an ill-kempt attempt at a goa-
tee. She usually liked facial hair on a man, but if the man
had been alive, it would have done nothing to enhance
his looks.

Cameron was definitely the better looking of the siblings. Beyond him identifying the remains as his brother's,
he hadn't told her much about the man on the floor before
them. She glanced toward the front of the house where Cameron was standing with Deputy Vetter, one of the younger
guys in their office.

Bullock cleared his throat, pulling her back to the question at hand.

"I would say he has been down at least four hours as
rigor mortis has begun to set in, based upon the state of
his hands and facial features."

"Good," Bullock said, nodding approvingly. "What else
do you notice?"

She wasn't sure what he wanted her to take note of, exactly, and she tried to follow his gaze. The man was wearing a dirty pair of jeans; mud was caked around the ankles.
The mud looked like the kind that came from tromping
around in the pasture on a wet day, yet the morning had
been relatively dry. He was wearing a highlighter-yellow,

road-worker-type work shirt that had faded oil stains throughout.

There was a long scar down the man's right arm and along it was a black jaguar tattoo, which made the cat appear as though it was prowling on the edge of some fleshy cliff if viewed from just the right angle.

"Do you see it?" Bullock asked.

"See what, Detective?"

He sent her a sly smile. "First," he led, "do you think this man is a victim of murder or suicide?"

From his toothy smile and the flicker of light in Bullock's eye, she felt as though she was walking into some kind of trap. "When I first entered, I would have said suicide. However, based on the position of his finger on the Glock's trigger, I'm thinking it's possible his hand was staged on the weapon."

Bullock's smile grew more wicked. "Is that right?"

"So, you think it was murder?"

"I'm not sure, but I would say that his death deserves further investigation."

Bullock put his hand on her shoulder. "Good job. That's a helluva an answer."

She had never thought of the detective as being on her side before, and certainly not as her friend. His warmth with her was throwing her for a loop, but it wasn't unwelcome. It was nice to have him willing to stand in her corner when it came to learning the craft of investigation—it was a skill set that could only be honed through hours of practice and hundreds of calls. Without officers like him—those who were willing to share their accrued knowledge—valuable experience and lessons were lost and it was the victims and their families who most felt the loss and pain of poorly trained and executed investigations.

"From what I figure," he continued, "based on our guy's temp, he's been down for at least four hours, but possibly more—like you said. Which means that these deaths likely occurred just before dawn."

"Rancher's hours. Makes sense."

Bullock nodded. "Whoever was behind these deaths knew the pattern of life on the ranch. Means that they were somehow connected. This wasn't just some stranger off the highway who popped in and randomly started attacking."

Truth be told, she hadn't even thought about something like that as a possibility. That, right there, was why he was the detective and, if she ever wanted to become one, it would take a heck of a lot of time.

"In cases like these, it is a safe bet to focus on the most obvious suspect—they are usually the one who is guilty of the crime. To me, I gotta say I think it's pretty cut and dry."

She was far from seeing these deaths as cut and dry. Two minutes ago, she had thought it likely it was a simple murder-suicide. "What do you think happened?"

He nudged his chin in the direction of the front door. "I think your boy out there, Cameron, is quite possibly behind this. He is the one with the means and the motivation to do something like this."

Emily stepped back, pressing her back against the wall, though she was fully aware that she shouldn't have been touching anything in the room. "What makes you think it's cut and dry?" She just couldn't follow the detective's line of thinking, it felt like such a leap.

She followed his gaze to the mantel over the fireplace at the heart of the room. On it sat a collection of family photos. They were all in matching oak frames. From right to left, there were pictures of Leonard and his wife, then with a baby, and a picture with another, another and another, until their images were showing flecks of gray hair at their temples and they had four grown children. Then the wife disappeared and Leonard looked noticeably wizened, deep crow's feet etching the corners of his eyes.

There were also pictures of each of the kids in their high school graduation gowns and of the girls graduating from the University of Montana. After that, the pictures ended—and it was as if the family had come to an end.

Her gaze drifted down to Ben's dead body.

If the family had been scattered to the wind before, the loss of the patriarch and the second brother would definitely do it no favors.

"From what I can make of things—" Bullock nudged his chin toward the photos "—Cameron and his sisters are going to be the ones who stand to inherit the ranch now that Leonard and the other brother are out of the way."

"Do you really think that's enough of a reason for him to commit murder? I wouldn't share a hairbrush with my sister let alone a ranch. Two sisters forced to share with him would only make it worse."

"True," Bullock agreed. "However, has anyone reached out to them? We also haven't seen the will. It wouldn't surprise me if the guy who owned this place was a little bit on the misogynistic side and wasn't the kind to leave land to a female child."

His statement struck a nerve, making her grit her teeth until her jaw ached. She hated that the problem was so widespread that Bullock had a fair point.

"From the looks of you and Cameron together, I would say you've built a pretty good rapport. Yes?" Bullock stepped toward her and gently pulled her away from the wall as though he had noticed her faux pas but instead of condemning her was happy to merely silently correct.

How could he be so kind and yet irritate her about misogyny and Cameron so much all at the same time?

"We do seem to get along," she admitted, though she wasn't sure she wanted to as she wasn't exactly sure where Bullock was leading her.

"Good. That's good." He gave her a smile that made it clear she was about to be voluntold a task. "I need you to run him downtown. Take him into our interview room. I want you to get him on camera. Get as much information as you can. If you get enough to charge him, I want you to place him under arrest."

Chapter Five

Emily sauntered toward them as Cameron sat with Deputy Vetter in front of the barn, watching. He felt like such a fool just sitting there, waiting for his fate to be sealed. There was nothing he could do, nothing he could say or not say, that could deliver him from this chaos.

He needed to call the ranch's attorney's and set everything in motion with the family's trust and getting all the bank accounts transferred over to just his name so no one could misallocate funds. He couldn't afford anything else going sideways.

He'd heard so many horror stories about family ranches going to rubble in the aftermath of its owner's demise. In one instance, a ranch a few miles down the road had had a million-dollar lien placed against it the day the owner died, for work that had supposedly taken place. There was no record of the work having been done, but there had been so much happening on the ranch and it had gone to probate for so long, that no one could prove otherwise. As it had stood, there were receipts from the company who'd placed the lien and the courts had sided with the company even though it was known on the street that the lien had been a money-grabbing scam by an out-of-stater who had seen an opportunity to falsely make a claim and win, and they had seized it.

The Trappers shouldn't be going to probate for anything, but there was always something when death came knocking—and that was natural deaths, not even considering deaths like those Cameron was dealing with. He had to make sure everything was legally taken care of so no one had time to do anything reckless.

Wait, it would look horrible if I did that before my father's body is even off the ranch.

Yet, just like any big circus—the show had to go on— bills had to be paid, the mortgage was due on the first of the month, which was just a few days away. Then there were all the other bills he was sure the ranch had hanging over its head, farriers, grain, gas, and they'd had just taken in one of their trucks for a new transmission.

Normally, his father had taken care of finances. He'd never let Cameron do the books, but now that would fall on his shoulders and he feared what he would be walking into.

What scared him most, if he had to admit it, wasn't what he was facing and what he knew had to be done—it was all the unknowns.

He couldn't wrap his head around it. Sure, they hadn't been the tightest family, but there wasn't the kind of animosity that would lead to something like this happening out of the blue. That was, unless his father hadn't been telling him everything. And that, that right there, was something that was entirely possible.

Leonard was the type of guy who'd loved to keep things close to the chest. It was a tale as old as time in the ranching community; they were tough as nails and he and those like him could handle anything that life threw their way with a level of quiet indifference and stoicism that rivaled the granite batholiths embedded in the belly of the Rockies.

There had been one year when he was growing up that a forest fire had swept through the back of the ranch and destroyed the summer range, killing hundreds of their livestock. At the time, their grandfather, Leo Sr., had still been alive and, together, the fathers had barely spoken a single word about the tragic disaster. Looking back, without his grandfather in control, Cameron was sure that the ranch and the family wouldn't have survived the storm.

It hit him: now he was at the helm of the ship. He was the only man in the family left standing. What was more, his ship was empty. Only he, two sisters in the wind and the ranch still remained.

Was this the future his grandfather had wanted? Had he hoped for something more for his family? Or was the ranch all that had mattered?

Just as his grandfather's voice came to his mind, Emily's feet came into view in the dirt in front of him. "Heya, Cam," she said like she was trying to sound friendly, but there was a tiredness to her tone that made him glance up to see if that same weariness could be found in her eyes. It was. "I know you wanted to get the other half of your cattle moved today, but unfortunately, I'm going to need to get more folks onto the ranch to continue our investigation. To do so, I'm going to need to run you downtown. You game?"

That sounded like a whole lot of words for her telling him that she needed to interrogate him.

His body tensed. "I didn't have anything to do with what I found."

She put her hand on his shoulder as though that would in some way make what she was saying better and less like a slap in the face. He pulled back and out of her touch. A flicker of rejection splashed over her features but was quickly masked by indifference. "I know you don't. We just need to talk. Come along with me." She motioned for him to stand up and she turned to have him follow.

He couldn't help but notice that her question had now turned into a command.

The younger deputy nodded in acknowledgment as he stood up. "Good luck, man. I'm sure I'll be seeing you later."

"Yep." He swallowed down the nerves creeping up from his stomach.

His boots crunched in the gravel as he made his way after Emily and he pulled down his cowboy hat just a little bit snugger on his forehead than he liked. Something about the pressure of it made him feel a touch more secure. He could handle this, her, the situation, all of it. If his grandfather could face a mass die-off and decimated property, he could handle answering questions about a situation in which he knew he was innocent.

At least there was some hope. She hadn't seemed upset with him, or like he was seriously a suspect. She just wanted to talk to him. Everything would be fine. All he had to do was go along with her.

His attempt to mollify himself was working right up to the point until they reached her patrol car and she opened the back door. He stared at the Plexiglas divider, which ran between the front seat and the hard plastic back seat where she motioned for him to sit.

He didn't know why he was surprised. Of course, he wouldn't be riding to the police station in the front seat. This wasn't a social visit. She was beautiful and he couldn't deny that he felt some strange desire for her, but that didn't make them friends. It didn't make them anything. In fact, on the surface, and from a logical point of view, he reminded himself that they were really enemies.

Climbing into the confinement of the back seat of the car, he was reminded of the last time he'd ridden in one. He'd been a senior in high school and Deputy Sutherland had picked him up for an MIP—minor in possession—at a kegger up the logging road near Lewis Trail. If he hadn't been drunk and passed out in the back of his best friend's pick-up, the guy would have never caught him.

However, as it was, it had probably been a good thing that the deputy had picked him up and taken him home, as he likely would have frozen to death otherwise. In the end, the judge had dropped the charges and he had gotten off with a slap on the wrist and fencing duties for a month from his father. Fencing had been far worse a sentence than anything the judge would have passed down. He still bore the scars from that summer's barbed wire on his hands.

Emily got in the car and they bumped down the rutted driveway and out toward the highway. They passed the pasture, where Bessie and Ginger were happily grazing on the green grass. Bessie gave a haughty swish of the tail as they passed by and it made him chuckle—at least one thing hadn't changed today.

"Do you need some air back there? I know it can get a little stuffy." Emily caught his gaze in the rearview mirror.

"Sure." She didn't need to keep up this fake friendship thing. No matter how she treated him, his statement wasn't going to change.

The air clicked on and a cool breeze passed over his skin. With it came the scent of dirt and grass pollen that had been caught in the air ducts of the car. It fluttered down and scattered over his blue jeans like ashes.

Emily sneezed in the front seat. "Bless you," he said instinctively.

She dabbed at her nose. "Thanks." She looked back at him. "Just so you know, you have the right to remain silent. You can also call your attorney at any time."

His heart clenched. "Are you placing me under arrest?"

She couldn't possibly... He hadn't given her any reason. He had just been at the wrong place at the wrong time. He had no reason to kill his brother or his father.

"No. I'm just making you aware of your rights. You are free to go at any time."

Free to go? Is she kidding? It wasn't like he could just jump out of her moving vehicle.

She had to know he was trapped.

"I thought you just wanted me out of the way. Why don't you just tell me the truth?" he asked, finally unable to play her game any longer.

"I am." She turned around as she came to a stop at the highway. "I'm just taking you to our offices for our convenience. It's the easiest place to question you about everything. I can get another person in the room with me this way as well."

He relaxed slightly as he looked at her worried expression. She had legitimately seemed concerned with him reacting as strongly as he had. Maybe she didn't think he was behind something nefarious after all.

She smiled at him and the strange attraction he felt toward her returned. Maybe he had overreacted in thinking she couldn't be his friend. Maybe she was trying to be his ally and help him make sense of everything. Maybe it was best that he left his father's death scene. It certainly hadn't seemed right sitting there, yards away from his body.

Emily hadn't said it, but she was doing him a favor.

His mind was just all over the place, and it was justifiable.

"I get it," he said, relaxing into the hard plastic seat. It pressed into the backs of his knees and made his jeans pinch his skin, but he didn't move and let the pain simply wash over him as the sensation was a welcome reprieve from the emotional waves he had been riding.

"I'm sorry that everything has to be this way," she said. She tapped on the steering wheel like she was playing some invisible drum.

Her candor surprised him. "I know that you're just doing your job. And I hope *you* know that I really didn't have anything to do with my father's or my brother's deaths. I don't hate my dad. And I wished neither of them harm. My dad and I actually got along pretty well. Sure, we had our fights, like I told you, but by and large we were friends. We had each other's backs, and we could rely on one another like no one else could. After my mother died, we were all that was left."

She let out a long exhale. "I know what it's like to experience that level of loss. It tends to reconfigure your life in a way that you just had no idea about or could expect."

"Yeah. We were moving forward well though. It has been quite a few years since my father had lost my mom and I thought he had moved past it. We were getting back on our feet, and the ranch was doing great. That was until the last couple of years, and he was saying he had gotten us in a little bit of debt, but something like that is not that uncommon for ranches. It's just part of the cycle."

"So, you'd say that there was some level of financial instability on the ranch?"

He paused, thinking about the note his father had taken

out and the piles of bills sitting on the desk in the main office. "Sure."

"Do you think that this debt could have had anything to do with what happened this morning?" She glanced at him in the mirror.

"My father wasn't great with money, but the only debt I know anything about for sure was that which he held with the banks. I don't see them coming out to kill him. It seems counterproductive to kill a man if they want to get their money back."

"You're right, but I'm sure I don't have to explain to you that, when it comes to money, damned near anything is possible." She tapped her finger on the wheel. "Did your father have any mental health issues that I need to know about?"

The question caught him off guard. Mental health wasn't something that was talked about in his family, no matter how much it probably should have been. Especially after the death of his mother and the resulting depression that his father had faced after her passing.

"He wasn't diagnosed with anything, but he had his ups and downs like everyone else. Lately, he had seemed like he had been more stressed, but when I talked to him about his shift in behavior, he hadn't wanted to open up."

"What do you mean by his *shift in behavior*?" she pressed, pulling down the main street, which led to the courthouse and the sheriff's office.

"He was antsy. Lots of phone calls and busier than usual. I'd been doing a lot of the day-to-day running of the ranch while he'd been doing more of the business side of things."

Emily made a tsking sound as she sucked on her teeth, and it made him tense. "Have you taken out any loans in your name on behalf of the ranch?"

His stomach sank as he realized how bad his owing the ranch and his father money could possibly look at this moment. "Yes. I had drawn money from the ranch account to pay off my ex-wife, April. We settled out of court, and I owed her seventy thousand dollars. My father floated me the money."

"Oh." Her sound was guttural and almost pained.

He hated it.

"I planned on paying him and the ranch back. I was working on it. I just needed to get back on my feet. It was why I was forced to stay here, to keep working the ranch."

"So, you didn't want to stay here?" Her voice suddenly had a harder edge, more coplike. "Your dad forced your hand with the money?"

The truth was that he had, but that wasn't the only reason Cameron had stayed. He loved the ranch. He had just grown up wanting something more than being a rancher whose life was dictated by the weather, politics and the fickle nature of beef prices. He wanted to tell her everything. He wanted to open up to the beautiful woman who smiled at him and whose eyes sparkled when she looked at him, but he couldn't talk to the cop who was now glaring back at him in the rearview mirror. Just like that, he had a feeling he had gone from being a possible suspect to one utterance away from wearing a set of glittering handcuffs.

He looked out at the redbrick building and the looming domed courthouse. He'd never really noticed it before, but all the windows on the main floor were covered with thick black steel bars, making it look eerily like a prison.

Maybe he had never noticed them before as he had never been a suspect in a murder—he had never had to worry that once he walked in, he may not walk out a free man.

Chapter Six

Emily stared at the red Ford F-150 that was parked near the front doors of the sheriff's office. Todd knew she was working, and he was aware that he wasn't to see her unless it was previously arranged or on their assigned parenting schedule. Yet, there was that damned pickup truck with the Rocky Mountain Elk Foundation specialty license plate and the cracked front windshield from the drive they took four years ago to Seattle.

He had been so angry that day. She had been running a little late with Stacy. Getting her ready had taken longer than expected as Stacy hadn't wanted to get dressed and had thrown a full-blown, body-flailing-on-the-floor, temper tantrum when Emily had tried to get her to put her clothes on. That had led to a spitting-food breakfast, which had led to a kitchen floor cleanup and a quick cry in the bathroom, none of which Todd had seen. When he'd walked in from packing the truck, he'd been on her and she had snapped at him, which had only made things worse.

Looking back, it was a good metaphor for their relationship—each had been blind to the needs and realities of the other and both had been angry and lashing out on the other. She hadn't been perfect, but Todd had been more than unkind—especially when he'd turned to Autumn Jessop to talk about what a bad wife and mother Emily was and would forever be. It hadn't taken long for them to fall into bed together and for her to find out.

As they neared the pickup and she pulled into her parking spot, she saw Todd sitting in the driver's seat. In the back, in her car seat, Stacy was thankfully fast asleep and didn't see the police car.

Why were they here?

Today wasn't Emily's day with her, and as badly as she wanted to scoop up her daughter and take her home, it wasn't convenient. Todd could see she was busy and had someone in her unit. He couldn't have possibly thought this was a good time to stop by, and yet there he sat.

As she came to a stop, she turned around to face Cameron in the back seat. "I'll need you to hang tight for a second. I need to deal with something really quick, and then we'll head inside." She jumped out of the car, not giving him time to respond or ask questions.

Todd was getting out of his pickup as she approached.

Even though it had only been a couple of weeks since the last time she had seen him out of his truck and without his hat, it seemed as though his hairline had receded even farther. Now, his dark chestnut hair was almost back to his ears. It wouldn't be long before he would be completely bald. His impending hair loss had always been a source of embarrassment to him. He'd tried every hair product to reduce hair loss known to man.

In fact, it was along those lines that she had found out about Autumn. One day, she had come home to find a pamphlet on the table for a hair transplant procedure out of Turkey. As desperate as he had been to keep his hair, he had told her he would never go that far. Apparently, that had changed when other women had entered the picture.

It brought her a little bit of joy to see that he was losing the battle. It was petty, she was aware, but after all she had been through with him, all the battles and war she had lost in the divorce, it was the little things—or hairs this time—that brought her a glimmer of joy.

"What are you doing here, Todd?" Annoyance filled her voice. "I'm working. You're not supposed to be here unannounced."

He rolled his eyes like a petulant teenager, as if she were the one who was acting out of line. "Look, I don't wanna be here and around you any more than you wanna be around me. However, something came up and I don't have anybody to watch Stacy. Even your stupid neighbor lady wasn't home. Penny or whatever her stupid name is."

If it had been the first time he had done this to her, she would have been slightly more patient with him, and yet this was the third time in the last six months that he had shown up in her life and had "an emergency" and couldn't take their daughter. Before, it hadn't been a problem, but the other times she hadn't been at work.

"Todd, I can't take her. I'm in the middle of a homicide investigation." She motioned toward her car where Cameron sat.

He was watching and as she looked his way he quickly glanced away. She couldn't begrudge him for watching her personal drama unfolding. It was completely unprofessional and out of line. Warmth rose in her cheeks even though she tried to control her embarrassment.

Todd looked over at Cameron and seemed unsurprised. "You must like having him in your back seat. You always had a thing for cowboys."

Her embarrassment was instantly replaced by rage.

She started to form her rebuttal but she checked herself.

It didn't do her any good to fight with Todd. He was just trying to get under her skin. In fact, making her angry and hurting her feelings might have been his favorite hobby—it sure had been when they had been together. She doubted some things ever changed.

When he seemed to realize he wasn't going to get a rise out of her, his shoulders slumped slightly and he turned to his back door and their daughter. She had fallen asleep. Her Mickey and Minnie Mouse ponytail holders were askew and most of her hair was stuck to the chocolate that was smeared all over her face.

"I told you I can't take her. I meant it, Todd." She moved to stop him from opening the door and waking up their child. She didn't want to upset Stacy by having her daughter wake up and see her and then think that—even for a second—Mommy didn't want her.

"You have to," he said, pushing past her and opening the door.

"Todd!"

"Kiddo, you gotta wake up. You're going with your mom."

She clenched her teeth so hard that they squeaked under the pressure. He was such an inconsiderate, manipulative jerk. It was always about Todd and what he needed—regardless of anyone else. This time, he was not only putting Emily's job on the line, but he was also quite possibly putting her daughter in danger.

Emily wanted to think that Cameron was a good man, everything in her heart told her he was, but she had fallen for Todd—clearly, when it came to men, she couldn't always be trusted.

Her first priority and her first concern had to be about the welfare and safety of her daughter.

"Where are you going that is so important, Todd?"

He said something that she couldn't hear as he pulled Stacy out of her car seat and sat her down on the ground. He grabbed her princess backpack and pushed it into Emily's hands. "Here, just take it." The pack was sticky and there was a glob of what looked like gum stuck to the front, it was complete with patches of dog hair and lint stuck in its pink gooey surface.

Stacy rubbed her fist in her eye and she smiled up at her with her sweet little toothy grin as she spotted her. "Hi, Mommy," she said in her cherubic, five-year-old, high-pitched voice.

"Hi, ladybug," she said, slipping her hand into her daughter's sticky hand. From this morning to now, there was no chance that her daughter had washed or brushed any part of her body and, based on her face, the only thing she had probably eaten was candy.

It had already been slated to be a long day, but having a sugared-up, potentially grumpy kiddo on her hands was a recipe for disaster. Looking at Stacy, though, there was no way she would let her go back with her dad. Emily didn't really like it when Stacy was with him for the few days he had custody of her and seeing her disheveled and unwanted reaffirmed her need to take her—no matter the consequences.

For now, her daughter could sit in the sergeant's office until she was done talking to Cameron or something.

She slung the backpack over her shoulder and then picked Stacy up and put her on her hip. As she turned to speak to Todd, he was already getting back in his pickup. He slammed the door in her face. He didn't even look back in their direction as he started the engine and tore off down the road, kicking up gravel as he hit the gas.

He knew her well enough that he had known she wouldn't say no to him leaving Stacy with her like this. When it came to her little ladybug, there was nothing she wouldn't sacrifice for her—and there wasn't anything stopping Todd from taking advantage, regardless of the parameters set forth by their mediated and agreed-upon parenting plan. It was on days like this that she was glad they were going back and renegotiating the damned thing.

Stacy snuggled into her, pressing her sweaty and sticky face into the crook of her neck. Her daughter smelled like stale cigarette smoke. She would need a bath tonight.

Emily turned toward the front doors of the office, where Cameron was sitting in her cruiser. He waved at Stacy and she could feel her daughter smile against her chest. She stuck up her hand in a grabby hand wave.

It tore at her that she would have to take her inside the office and hand her off to go into a full-blown interview, all while the office would be in a tither about her bringing in her daughter to work and expecting them to babysit. Of course, they would all be sweet and accommodating to her face, but behind her back, it would be an entirely different story.

Katie, the woman who worked at the front desk, loved to stir the pot. If there wasn't something going on in the office, she would find some kind of drama to start. This would be just the sort of thing she loved to sink her teeth into and use against someone in perpetuity.

Though Emily couldn't prove it, she was almost positive Katie wrote down everyone's secrets and flaws so if she needed ammunition to blackmail or start something, she could go to her little black book—most in the office called her the Crypt Keeper for that very reason.

Katie wore big, black-rimmed glasses that made her

look a little bit like Edna Mode on *The Incredibles*, and the thought of walking in and having Katie gaze at her over the top of those stupid glasses while judging away made her stomach churn. Between that look, the gossip and the judgment, she realized the last place she wanted to be was inside that building. She could question Cameron anywhere. If anything, maybe she could get him to open up more if she treated him like a friend instead of a suspect.

Besides, he had just lost his brother and his father. From the time she had spent with him, he didn't seem like the type who would have committed this crime as Bullock had assumed. In fact, based on his body language and the way he spoke about the event, she was convinced he was innocent. And if what she assumed was correct, and he had nothing to do with their deaths, he needed to have a safe place to turn.

Emily stopped beside Cameron's door. She opened the door and Cameron stepped out, slicked down his hair and put on his dirty white cowboy hat.

"Hiya, cutie," he said, leaning down slightly so he could be at Stacy's level where she was snuggling.

His greeting made her instantly like him a bit more. Most men she knew were standoffish or in a rush to hand off kids—Todd as example number one.

Stacy squirmed and pushed off her, moving to be put down. Emily was surprised, but she put her daughter on her feet and took her by the hand. Normally, Stacy was shy when it came to new people, and especially men. When she had met Todd's brother, it had taken her two weeks before she would even look at him when he talked to her.

"I'm Stassy," she said, holding her *s*, thanks to her wiggling front tooth, and extending her chubby hand like a mini-adult but squeezing Emily's extra hard for reassurance.

"Very nice to meet you, Ms. Stacy. I'm Cam," Cameron said, taking her hand and giving it a gentle shake. He got down on one knee and bowed before her. He took off his cowboy hat before pressing his forehead to the top of her hand like a knight paying homage to a princess.

She giggled and the sound brought a smile to Emily's lips. The man knew his way to all the ladies' hearts.

He stood up.

"Did you eat yet, ladybug?" she asked.

She shook her head. "I'm hungry."

Looking at how much chocolate she had on her, it was no wonder. The sugar rush had probably worn off and left a pit in her stomach. She'd need to feed her daughter before she got grumpy or there would be all hell to pay. "Do you mind if we grab some lunch?" she asked Cameron.

It felt strange, breaking so far from what they were supposed to be doing, but she had to make the best of a bad situation and she had to be the queen of the pivot.

He smiled. "Anything is better than that back seat."

Her daughter couldn't take her eyes off the brunette cowboy as he slipped his hat back over his curly locks. Emily didn't want to admit it, but she could completely understand Stacy's desire to stare at the man. He was undeniably handsome with those sky-blue eyes that seemed even brighter than they had this morning thanks to the sun. His face was tan and when he smiled, it made the little lines around his eyes collect at the corners and lead like road maps to the center of his soul.

"Are you coming with us, Cam?" her daughter asked, tilting her head ever so slightly.

Cameron glanced over at Emily and she gave him a

nod. "Is it okay with you if I tag along with you and your beautiful mama?"

"You better. You need to eat. You're a growing boy." Stacy put her hands on her hips and frowned up at him.

He laughed. "Well then, it sounds like I have my marching orders."

He reached his hand out for Stacy's and she slipped her little hand into his tanned fingers. She let go of her mother and skipped forward as she and Cameron started to walk toward the heart of town where all the diners and cafés could be found.

Beautiful? She stood watching the duo walking ahead of her as she tried to make sense of his compliment.

He had to have just been being nice for the benefit of making friends with her daughter. It was definitely in his best interest to want to get in good with her and Stacy. It would make his life immeasurably easier—in fact, it already had. It had saved him from being sucked into the belly of the courthouse.

Or, what if he'd meant it? What if he really did think she was beautiful?

The thought made her blush.

Emily had never really thought much about her looks after high school. She had her routines, and she took care of herself, making sure she did her hair and makeup every day, but beyond that—it was just habit.

As she moved to follow behind them, she caught a glimpse of her reflection in the windshield. She straightened her shirt and fixed a hair that had fallen loose of her hair tie and was flagging in the light breeze.

Surely, he was just being nice, but it was flattering. It had been a long time since anyone had treated her as anything but a coworker or a pain in their rear end. It was nice to be reminded that she was still seen as something more than just a mom or a cop—he saw her as a woman.

Cam looked back over his shoulder at her and sent her a wilting smile as her daughter started to skip. For a moment, Emily nearly forgot where she was and what she had been sent there to do. Instead, all she could think about was what it would be like to have a world like this with a cowboy like him, and a beautiful and loving family.

It was just too bad her dreams never seemed to become reality.

Chapter Seven

Cameron had always had a way with children, but things had come even more naturally with Stacy. He couldn't explain why, but the two of them had taken an instant liking to each other and all the way through lunch the little girl hadn't stopped talking to him. Emily had seemed a touch standoffish at the beginning of the meal, or perhaps it was that she had other things on her mind—he would have, if he had been in her shoes, given the little performance her ex had put on there in the road outside the cop shop.

He felt bad for her. That guy had put her in one hell of a position.

Cam didn't blame Emily for not wanting to drag him and her little girl into the office. He could only imagine how it would have been received. It was cute when a dad brought a little kid into the office, but not so much if they dropped them off for a whole day of babysitting.

He sipped on his last bit of coffee in the heavy brown coffee cup, reminiscent of former days, as the girls made their way to the restroom to wash hands after their chicken strips. He stared down at the place mat with his and Stacy's red crayon drawing of a stick-figure pirate with a parrot on his shoulder and his sword drawn. The silly picture made him smile.

He'd never given much thought about being a father.

His ex-wife hadn't wanted children and been adamant about their not getting pregnant; he hadn't pressed the issue at the time.

Thank goodness, they hadn't had children. It would have made his decision to divorce so much harder. It had been hard enough as it was. Even with her infidelity, he'd still loved April. He could have forgiven her, but he couldn't have forgotten. She had broken his heart and when he had found out, he'd known he would never be able to trust a woman again.

He stared down at the pirate.

Emily wasn't like most women; she was a law enforcement officer. Their entire lives were built on trust and honor. Their word was their bond. Without integrity, they were nothing.

He picked up the red crayon and started to color in the blade of the sword as he thought about Emily's strikingly blue eyes. They were almost the same shade of blue as his, but there was a hint of brown around their centers. Wasn't that called hazel?

As he colored the knife, his mind wandered to her standing by his father's body and the knife protruding out of his father's chest. The Ruana.

He pulled his phone out of his pocket and opened his gallery. Tapping on his photos, he pulled up the picture he had taken of his father's body resting against the back tire of the pickup truck. He zoomed in on his dad. It was macabre, but he realized he hadn't really looked closely at the knife.

It was probably nothing, but it seemed strange to him that it was his father's knife that had been used to kill him. His father had loved that knife, and it had been one of his most prized possessions. If someone had wanted to really put it to him, that was the weapon they would have wanted to use to do the job.

Or, if it wasn't a premeditated thing, it would have just been convenient. Maybe the killer had run into his father outside and gotten into a fight. His father had probably drawn it, and the guy had fought it out his father's hands. Maybe.

What about Ben though? If Ben had been behind his father's death, why would he have taken his own life? Why wouldn't he have just committed suicide by his father? And why wouldn't he have just shot his father if he'd wanted him dead?

So many things about what had happened, and the order of events, confused him. Nothing seemed to line up.

As he gazed at the picture, he looked down at his father's belt. The knife sheath was empty.

He swiped to the picture he had taken of Ben through the window. In the photo, Emily was crouching down beside his brother's body. There was an orb of light thanks to the reflection of his flash in the window and it obscured the area around his brother's feet, but he could make out the gun and his brother's hand.

He didn't recognize the gun as one of his or his father's, so it must have been one Ben had purchased after he had left the place; or maybe it wasn't his at all.

He just couldn't make sense of why his brother would have brought a gun to the ranch in the first place. His father and his brother hadn't been fighting, at least that Cam had known about. His dad normally let him in on big things, and he hadn't even mentioned Ben as of late. Everything they had been dealing with was the day-to-day running of the place and the ever-evolving debt that his father had often complained about.

Stacy came running up and slid belly-down into the seat next to him then wiggled back up into a sitting position. She picked up her fork and started eating more of the french fries that she had left on her plate.

"You all set?" Emily asked. "We still need to talk, but I need to get her home and start her bedtime routine. She's normally asleep by 7:30."

Was she asking him back to her place?

He tried to check his look of surprise. "Let's hit it." He leaned toward Stacy. "You ready, kiddo?"

Stacy popped another fry into her mouth and she nodded, sliding out from the bench seat.

She slipped her hand into his; it was still damp from the bathroom, but he didn't mind. He liked the feeling of her little starfish fingers in the center of his palm. He liked knowing she was safe with him and, unlike the guy—who Emily had told him was a dude named Todd, her ex-husband and Stacy's dad—who had just dropped her and run earlier in the day, he wouldn't just leave her without warning.

Todd had seemed like a real piece of work. He couldn't understand what Emily had ever seen in the dude. Even from a distance, he'd looked like a loser. And what guy would just drop his kid off at a police station when he could clearly see that Cameron was in the back of her patrol car—even if *he* was not really a problem?

The dude was a peach.

He had to remind himself that his opinion of her ex-husband and her life didn't really matter. He wasn't her boyfriend. Heck, they weren't even really friends. This was just some strange life-required pause in her interrogation of him.

The only good news was that if she really thought he

was behind any the deaths, he doubted she would have allowed for their wavering from protocol. His butt would have been in some holding cell by now or something; he didn't really know how the whole cop and questioning thing worked. All he knew was what he had seen on shows, and even when it came to that, he didn't watch a whole lot of television.

They walked out of the restaurant, but instead of heading toward her patrol car, they turned in the other direction and walked down the dirt alley behind the Coffee Cup. Their footfalls crunched in the dirt and broken glass that littered the alley, but the girls didn't seem to notice.

Stacy's hand started to sweat in his in the summer heat and he slowed down his pace in an effort to keep in step with her. Emily took her other hand and looked over at him. Stacy looked up at them and smiled, but under her eyes were dark circles.

She really was a cute kid.

Emily stopped at a gate in a chain-link fence around a white farmhouse-style, two-story house. It was decorated with black shutters and at its peak there were black Victorian pediments with incredibly elaborate scrollwork. The house was antiquated but well kept and the yard was beautifully maintained.

"Is this your house?" he asked, unable to hide the surprise in his voice.

He wasn't sure why he was surprised. Of course, she would have a place as beautiful and put together as her. Yet, if he had envisioned her home, it would have been something modern. Minimalist but classy and high-end. She would have the best of things but understated. A little bit of everything.

She couldn't have been all those things. As he thought

about it as they walked to the front door and she unlocked it, he realized how much his characterization didn't make sense. But then it did: she was just a collection of contrasts.

He tried not to stare at her ass as she bent down to pick up Stacy and place her on her hip. Her utility belt cut into her waist and the grip of her gun dug into her side thanks to the weight of the little girl on the other side. But Emily didn't seem to notice. She must have been the primary caregiver.

The woman worked her tail off. He appreciated that in another person.

He followed the girls inside and Emily led him to her living room. At its center was a large leather sofa, the kind that came from specialty furniture stores where even the lamps were hundreds of dollars and only the wealthy and interior designers shopped.

The entire room was in style with the sofa. Warm and welcoming, beckoning to be noticed. It was all as classy as she was.

Emily took Stacy upstairs and, after a quick bath— complete with giggles—put her daughter to bed. While he waited, he clicked through the pictures from this morning on his phone.

The stairs creaked as Emily made her way downstairs and back to him. "Sorry about that. She just does best when I keep her on her bedtime routine."

He clicked off his screen and put his phone down. "It's all good. We all do best with our routines, I get it."

Emily walked by him and sat down in the leather recliner, which seemed to fit her body like it had been sculpted for her. She must have spent many nights rocking Stacy to sleep in the thing. It made him feel things he hadn't felt in a long time, not since he had been married. Being around her so much made him miss that feeling of not just comradery and partnership, but of a deep sense of home and belonging—and what he missed most, love.

Not that he loved her. It was just that he missed the sensation and connection that came with being loved and loving another.

Until now, he hadn't really considered getting into another relationship again—and certainly not getting married.

"I know it's unconventional, all of this," she said, motioning around her house.

"You mean bringing a suspect in a potential murder-suicide investigation back to your house?" He laughed, relaxing back into the seat on the couch.

Or a double homicide, the jury is still out, he thought.

"If I was worried that you actually had something to do with your father's and brother's deaths, I would have never even considered bringing you here, or having you around my daughter."

He thought about the look she had given him when Todd had handed off Stacy and she had walked over and let him out of the car. It had been in that moment when she had made her decision. She had a hell of a lot more faith in humans than he did, but he was thankful that, in this case, her faith was well-placed in him.

"I'm honored." He dipped his head in sincerity.

"That being said, Detective Bullock needs to pin this on someone, and he wanted me to place you under arrest if you gave me any indication that you were behind this. When it comes to the public, when there are homicides, the next thing we field is mass fear that it will happen to them. People fear the boogeyman in the night."

"I am the one who should be afraid. For all I know, someone out there who may want the men in my family dead," he said, not even thinking about what he was saying until it had already escaped his mouth. Yet, as soon as he had said it, he realized how right he was.

She stared at him, her eyes wide as though she, too, hadn't thought about the legitimacy of his statement before now, either. "Do you have any idea who could be behind this?"

He shook his head. "I've wracked my brain. The only thing I've come up with is my ex-wife, the bank my dad borrowed money from and whomever my brother was tied up with. None of it really makes sense to me though. My ex and I don't really have anything to do with each other and I bought her out. We haven't talked since."

"Do you have access to all the ranch's financial records?" she asked, but there was a strange expression on her face—bordering on mischievous.

She was sexier than ever.

"I'm sure I can pull them up, but my dad was the one in control of everything." He stared at her hazel eyes, not so long as to make things weird but he couldn't look away from her playful expression.

"I can't look at those records without getting a search warrant and going through Detective Bullock."

He didn't mind saving her work. In fact, if there was anything he could do to speed up their investigation and figure out who was behind the deaths, the better. It made him feel exposed, knowing that there was someone out there who wanted his family, and possibly him, dead. But did they really want him dead? It was a strange feeling not to know for sure.

If they wanted him dead, they could have just stayed

a little bit longer and waited for him to arrive, and they could have killed him just as easily as they had killed Ben and his father. That was if they knew that he was set to arrive. Maybe they'd been interrupted, maybe somebody had shown up on the ranch or they had gotten scared.

There were so many things running through his mind. He also wanted to know about her relationship with Detective Bullock. They had appeared to get along, which seemed strange. Being a woman in a small-town sheriff's office couldn't have been easy. It hadn't looked as though they'd had a relationship beyond friendship, but he had no idea.

"I know this is coming out of nowhere, but I just have to ask, is anybody going to walk through that door tonight and be upset that I am here?" He motioned toward the front door.

The mischievous look on her face disappeared. "No, the last man I had in my life—and I hate to admit this—was Todd. And you can see how well that went between us."

He bit the inside of his cheek to stop his smile. He didn't want her to misread it.

"I didn't want to talk to you about him in front of Stacy too much, but he has a tendency to take advantage of me when it comes to her. He isn't a nice man. And if he wasn't her father, I probably would have never stayed here."

That was the only reason he could be grateful for the guy's existence. "I'm glad you stayed. As for marrying him, we all make mistakes in our lives." He paused. "I like to think of first marriages like a pancake, it never comes out quite right. Most end up in the trash."

She laughed, and it made his heart lighten. He didn't know how much he had needed that until now.

He wanted to know what Todd had done to hurt her, but

at the same time in this single moment he could tell that she needed to relax and take comfort in levity as badly as he did. They both hated Todd, only the fervor with which Cameron couldn't stand the guy would change with more information. And even that was debatable as, right now, he couldn't care less if the guy lived or died. Stacy and Emily both deserved better in their lives.

Emily's phone pinged with a message. She opened it up and her face darkened as she read whatever was on the screen.

"Is everything okay?" he asked.

She didn't seem to hear him as she typed away in response to the message. After a few more pings, she finally looked up. "Did you say something?"

"You okay?" he repeated.

She nodded. "That was the detective. They're holding the bodies until morning, and I will need to come back and write up my reports. He's leaving the scene for tonight, but they have an officer holding it." She stared at her phone, but he could tell that she really wasn't looking at it and was just zoning out.

"Did he find anything of interest?"

She looked at him, a haunted expression upon her face. She said nothing for a long moment. Whatever was bothering her, she didn't want to tell him.

"Just tell me. Whatever it is, it's okay."

She blinked then pinched her lips together before taking a long breath. "Your father..."

"Yes?"

She reached over to him and put her hand on his knee. Under most circumstances, her warm touch would have been a comfort but now he found it disconcerting. "His fingerprints were all over the gun found in your brother's hand. Bullock thinks it's possible he was the one to pull the trigger."

Chapter Eight

It was strange how quickly someone could move from being a stranger to being a friend. Emily couldn't have pinpointed the exact moment when she'd gone from looking at Cameron like a major suspect to the man she now was attempting to comfort, but here they were.

She stared at her fingers on his thigh and felt the warmth radiating up through his jeans. It tore at her that she had to tell him about the possibility that his father could have played a role in his brother's death. Yet, it still didn't make heads or tails of how his father had come to be stabbed outside by the truck—or why his father would have staged the gun in his brother's hand.

It was just a lead, but it made things a whole lot more complicated.

Cameron reached down with his left hand and put it on top of hers. He didn't look at her and instead reached over to the phone beside him on the couch with his free hand and started tapping away on the screen. She tried not to move her fingers beneath his.

The motion of his putting his hand on hers had seemed to come so naturally to him, like they had been dating forever and it was just a typical Tuesday night—and yet, she was in the power role. However, was she really? She had given up any professionalism the moment her daughter had arrived, and she had driven the nail in the coffin when she had told him about Todd and her relationship status.

He didn't seem to be aware of the feelings amassing within her, but she was glad.

He looked up from his phone's screen. "According to Stockman's Bank, we were running lean. Which he had told me." He moved closer to the side of the couch to be closer to her and so she could see his phone.

As he moved, her hand fell away from his leg. Where his hand had been on hers started to chill and she wanted to reach out and put his hand back, but it was best to leave things as professional as possible. She had already crossed enough lines; there was no point in going past anymore. If they had a relationship now, it could be disastrous at several levels—starting with the investigation and moving all the way to how it would affect Stacy.

She looked down at the bank account records. There were payments to what appeared to be the mortgage company, electric, the ranch supply store, gas stations and the grocery store. She motioned to touch his phone and he answered with a simple nod. She scrolled up. Near the middle of the month, on the fifteenth, was a seventeen-thousand-dollar charge. "Do you know what this is for?"

He shook his head. "No idea. This is my dad's account."

There was a series of large cash deposits, one every week and sometimes twice. "Didn't you say you guys were struggling for funds?" She did some quick math. "According to what I'm seeing here, just in cash deposits, your father was depositing more than forty-thousand dollars a month. Then you have what looks like your cattle sales and your regular business profits that go through your corporate name."

"Forty thousand? There is no way." He jerked back his phone and clicked through each month like she couldn't have possibly been right. Yet, as he slowed down, she could see it click that what she had said was accurate. "It... This doesn't make sense. We had to take out loans for our new equipment. We were scraping by."

"Yes, it looks like your father was spending almost that same amount each month. It seems like *huge* amounts of money were going to odd number-based points of sales—probably websites or something web-based. Do you know what your father could have been spending that much money on each month?"

He looked completely at a loss. "I told you everything I know about. We have a huge debt on a new machine we got last year. If we had this kind of money, where my dad could just piss it away like this on the internet, I can't believe he wouldn't have first paid off that machine. It's at eight percent interest. It's insane."

"But you admit your father is terrible with money?"

"Definitely." He exhaled, hard. He dropped his phone on the couch and then dropped his head into his hands, rubbing his temples. "None of this is making any sense—my brother being here, my father making and spending that kind of money, and why they ended up dead."

"We will figure it out." She stood up and walked over to him, sitting down next to him on the couch. She put her hand on his shoulder and leaned closer until their legs touched. It was a simple touch, but warmth radiated between them like shared breath. "But your dad wasn't selling drugs or anything, was he?" she teased with a laugh to lighten the mood.

"The closest thing my dad ever got to drugs was chewing tobacco and drinking beer—he did like his Banquets."

He smiled at what must have been the memory. "In fact, it's fair to say most of the charges at the gas stations were probably for a tank of gas, Copenhagen and a case of beer." He reached up and put his hand on hers.

"Then he was a true Montana rancher." She smiled at him as he stroked the back of her hand with his thumb.

He caught her gaze and she couldn't look away. Those eyes. Those incredible eyes. If she looked into them long enough, she was sure she would fall in. Like they were the depths of an ancient lake and the way to survive drowning was to swim straight to the island that was his heart. She had to hope that it wasn't completely made of stone.

"I wanted to say thank you." He took her hand in his and moved it toward his mouth. She could feel the warmth of his words on her fingertips, making parts of her awaken that had long been dormant.

"Thank me for what?" she asked, her sound airy thanks to the sensations coursing through her body and threatening to take over whatever control she had on her thoughts and abilities to speak.

"For believing in me. You didn't know me. You took a chance in believing in me. I will do everything I can to prove to you that you made a good choice—that I'm a man worth your faith." The way he spoke made her feel like he wasn't just talking about her case anymore.

He leaned forward and his lips brushed against the skin of her fingers.

"I...I believe you. I want to help you." She watched his lips connect with her hand and she grew impossibly wet as the heat of his mouth brushed over her skin. "We should go upstairs."

He looked up from his kiss and smiled at her, a sexy half smile that spoke of all the things she imagined him doing to her. She wanted to move in close and kiss those lips. They were so plump and she could imagine how they would feel on her tongue. He probably tasted like peppermint gum with a touch of salty man—and the flavor that made him *him*. If she had to bet, he probably tasted just as good as he smelled.

She moved slightly nearer, half afraid that she was reading this all wrong and he would jerk back and call her out for making a move. She drew in a long breath, pulling his manly scent deep into her lungs. He smelled like the ranch—fresh air mixed with hay and sweat. His scent was mixed with the aromas of the day and it made a heady concoction. She could actually feel her pupils dilate as her desire for him raced through her body.

Like he could feel how much she wanted him, he started to move toward her until she could almost feel his lips press against her. He was so close. Their eyes locked and she smiled at him.

He reached up and freed her hair from her ponytail, letting it cascade down her shoulders. He loosened her hair gently before moving his fingers up the back of her scalp. She leaned her head into his palm, letting him control her. It felt so good.

He moved her close, and he took her mouth with his.

The kiss. It was everything.

His thumbs moved up her face by her ears as he took control of her completely with both hands. His fingers moved through her hair. It was so sensual as his tongue flicked against hers and their flavors mixed.

She had been right—he tasted just as she had imagined, but if anything, it was better than she had expected. He tasted like ambrosia and the nectar of the gods that she had read about in her college English classes. She felt goddess-like now, springing to life in his hands like a flower that had been waiting for the sun's rays to come to full bloom.

Her hands found his chest and she moved back from his lips just slightly to look him in the eyes, to see if he was feeling what she was feeling. His eyes were heavy with lust and wanting.

There was a creak of the floorboards and she paused. After a few seconds, there was the sound of footfalls and the squeak of the third step.

Emily pulled away, out of Cameron's touch. She instantly hated it, but as she settled back into the couch, Stacy's ruffle-haired head appeared around the corner of the bottom of the stairs.

"Mommy?" she said, her voice sounding tired.

"Yes, ladybug?"

"Can Cam read me a story?" she asked, looking at Cameron who was smoothing down his hair.

He smiled at her and then slapped his knees as he stood up. "You got it, kiddo. What do you want? *Peter Rabbit* or *The Wizard of Oz*?"

There was no way her daughter had heard either of either of those classics, but Stacy smiled widely. "You pick."

As he walked off and took Stacy by the hand, Emily's disappointment disappeared and was replaced by a renewed sense of hope for her and her daughter's future.

Chapter Nine

He was a kid addict. Though he had never thought it would happen, he had fallen head over heels in love with Stacy. That kid was the cutest thing he had ever seen and, if given the chance, he would do anything to keep her safe—and that was to say nothing about her mother.

Now when it came to Emily, he couldn't say it was love, but that kiss… He couldn't think of a kiss that had ever been hotter—not even in the movies.

She was so far out of his league that he didn't even understand why she had kissed him in the first place. Or had he kissed her?

Last night and yesterday had been such a blur of activities and emotions that it didn't even feel like it could have all been real. Why was it that life could sometimes seem like it would go by so slowly and then suddenly everything would happen all at once?

Emily was over at her neighbor's, who had agreed to watch Stacy for the day while she went to work. The neighbor, an older retired woman named Penny, was apparently Stacy's normal caregiver and hated Todd just as much as he did—at least from what little he had overheard from her and Emily's phone call that morning. He'd listened while Stacy was eating her pancakes—complete with blueberries, which had left little seeds stuck up in her gums until her mom had made her brush her teeth.

While he waited, he went back to his phone and pulled up the bank records. As he went deeper into them, he noticed there were several to the big-rig company—Goemer's Diesel—that the WGC used for their truck parts. They kept two eighteen-wheelers on-site to haul cattle around the ranch and to sales when they needed. The rigs were old and had a habit of breaking down whenever they were actually needed. Cam had been planning on using one yesterday to move the cows up to the summer pasture.

When he'd gone to start the damned thing, Old Red, he'd called it, he'd found the alternator had gone out. He'd called the shop and ordered another one. It was probably ready to be picked up by now.

He ran his hand over his face as he thought about the cattle. They still needed to be moved. He also needed to get back to the ranch to feed the horses and make sure everything was taken care of for the morning. By now, the animals were probably getting antsy.

Bessie, the sassy horse, was definitely going to give him an earful when he got there.

Emily came strolling in the house. "You certainly know the way to a girl's heart, don't you?"

He put his phone away. He wanted to ask her if he knew his way to hers, but he bit his tongue. They had stopped at a good place last night, before things had gone too far and there was no going back. As much as he was attracted to her and he wanted things to progress, they couldn't be together. She was the cop investigating his father's and brother's murders. Until things were cleared and he was no longer a suspect at all, it felt wrong that they would be romantically involved.

He didn't want to compromise Emily, her investigation or her career.

"Your daughter is a sweetheart. You've done a really good job with her. You should be proud."

"I'm a long way from the home stretch, especially when it comes to things with her dad. However, thank you. I appreciate it. I don't hear that very often."

"I bet you don't." He felt awkward about saying that, and wished he hadn't, but he didn't know exactly why.

She cleared her throat, like she was feeling just as awkward as he was. "So, I need to look into all the leads today." She looked at the couch where he had piled up the blankets and stacked the pillows neatly from where he'd ended up last night. "Did you think of anything else while you were trying to sleep?"

"I just need to get back to the ranch, would that be okay? I know that the scene is still off limits, I don't wanna be around my father or brother. I just need to get in and take care of the animals."

Her smile disappeared. She nodded. "That shouldn't be a problem. Detective Bullock is already on his way there. Vetter has been there for an hour, and he relieved the deputy who was holding the scene for us last night. Just so you know, we are hoping to get the bodies out of there today. Do you have a funeral home that you would like to work with?"

Just like that, he came crashing back to reality and all the endorphins and happiness he had been feeling dissipated. There was so much to do. So many choices to make. So much chaos to deal with.

"Just use Gardiner Brothers. Cremation is fine. And I'm sure that we'll have to do autopsies, that's fine." He nodded, absentmindedly, trying not to think of their bodies being cut open on some cold stainless-steel table in a morgue somewhere.

She walked over to him. For a moment, he thought she was going to put her hand on him to comfort him, but she stopped short. It was as if she knew that what had happened last night was as far as they should take things as well. "Let's go."

She led the way to the door and waited for him to go outside before locking the door behind them. For a minute, he looked for their car outside and then remembered that they had parked by the diner. They walked in silence through the alley and around the block to her car. The town was already humming with tourists who were window-shopping along the little downtown area.

There was a rock and mineral shop and the door opened with the jingle of a bell; from inside he could hear kids laughing and talking. Farther down was an ice cream and espresso shop that had a line for morning coffees. Most of the people in line were plain women with huge purses and oversize hats, holding cell phones and tapping away instead of looking at the beautiful mountains surrounding them.

He let Emily walk in front of him and he watched the swish of her hips as she moved in her uniform pants. From under her shirt, around her middle, there was a thick band where yesterday he'd noticed she was carrying another gun in front. He wanted to know why she carried two guns, but then again, it made sense that she did.

If he was a law enforcement officer, he would have wanted to double carry as well. In their line of work, there was no room for gun malfunctions. If something happened and they lost use of their weapon, it would be terrifying. The old adage *Don't bring a knife to a gunfight* came to mind.

On the other hand, he hadn't heard of anyone in the area being part of an officer-involved shooting at any time in the recent past. Hopefully, she had never been in a situation where she had been forced to use her weapon on a civilian.

Instead of leading him to the back door of her patrol unit, as she had yesterday, she opened the passenger's-side door and smiled at him. He climbed in, and she didn't even close the door behind him. Instead, she let him close the door himself. He took it as a sign of major progress.

They made small talk about Stacy and her preschool as they headed for the ranch. According to Emily, Stacy was looking forward to starting kindergarten in the fall, and she had been reading for a year. She hadn't needed to tell him the last part. When he'd read to her last night, she had taken over for him on several occasions when he hadn't given Winnie the Pooh enough inflections in his voice.

The thought brought a smile to his face just as they pulled up to the yellow caution tape the sheriff's office had strung up around the crime scene that was his family's ranch.

He let out a long exhale as he got out of the car. Emily smiled over at him. It was a conciliatory smile, the kind that promised that things would get better, but they both knew it was something she couldn't guarantee.

The detective was already on scene and he made his way over to them. "How's it going?" He looked directly at Cam, like he was trying to decide whether or not Emily's faith in him was well-deserved.

"Good," Emily said, taking the helm. "We made some progress on the financial records. I'm going to look into that a little bit today, if that's okay with you?"

The detective looked him up and down before turning his attention to his deputy. "Yes, that would be fine." He nodded approvingly. "I got the judge to sign off on the warrant and the bank is working on getting us the official records. In the meantime, I have reached out to the FBI regarding the online charges and both men's cell phone records. When the warrant comes through, we will get them everything they need. You can take point on that. Good?"

Emily nodded.

Seeing her in action was a turn-on and it actually took Cameron off guard. He thought she was sexy before, but seeing a woman in a powerful alpha role was hot. It also made him wonder if they could get along if they dated. They were both type A personalities in a lot of ways. They were bound to butt heads.

Then again, he was putting the cart in front of the horse. Just because they'd kissed didn't mean they were going to be on the relationship wagon.

Cameron walked over toward the barn. He tried not to look at his dad's pickup, where he knew his father was still resting. He couldn't help but wonder how long his father could sit out there before he would start to really decay. By now, the flies must have started to come to the body. With cows, flies showed up almost as soon as the animal died. It was almost impressive how fast.

He went into the barn, grabbing hay and dropping it into the horses' stalls one by one until they were all taken care of. For the most part, this time of year, the horses were fine grazing, but he still liked to give them a little bit of hay, especially since today he wouldn't be able to turn them out like he normally would.

Next, he set about getting the pellets and grain mixtures together with the mineral powders and oils for each horse. Each animal took something a bit different, based on their nutritional needs thanks to their age, weight and breed.

Bessie, of course, was the most finicky and wouldn't eat anything with too much alfalfa.

She really was a pain. Yet, she was the one who had first alerted him to his father's passing.

What was he going to do with her now that his father was gone? She was wholeheartedly his horse. Cameron sighed as she walked up and put her head over the door of the stall and watched as he mixed her grain bucket. "Hey, pretty lady." He swirled the mix, poured it into her black feeder bucket and walked to her. She blew out as he neared, clearly impatient that he had taken so long to get her breakfast today.

"I know, I know. I got it though." He smiled, running his hand over her forehead. "You are just about as patient as Dad."

Or as Dad was, he silently corrected himself.

He slid the bucket into the stall and Bessie tore into the food like she hadn't been fed in a month. She was so dramatic sometimes. He looked her over while she ate. Luckily she didn't appear to have any ill-effects or rub marks from where the saddle had sat askew on her yesterday while she had run amok on the ranch.

He followed suit with the rest of the horses, finishing with Ginger, his bay. She was gentle and sweet and rested her head on his shoulder as he bent over to put her grain under the slat in her door. He caressed her, holding her head against him, and petted her with his eyes closed for a long minute. Sometimes, especially in moments like this, he wondered if animals could sense things beyond just happy and sad.

Of course, they could pick up on emotions; that was documented. But in this case, when he was so overwhelmed, could she sense how confused he was? From the way she nuzzled him, it seemed like she knew and wanted to help with it all.

He loved the animal.

There had been other horses he had been close to in the past. In many ways, they were like dogs, but larger and smarter. He'd had Ginger since she'd been born on the ranch fifteen years ago. He'd been there the night she'd arrived, and he'd nursed her through colic when he'd thought they'd lose her for sure. When she'd gotten healthy, he'd worked to break her and train her for driving cattle and trail riding in the fall.

She was his horse through and through. And more, he could have ridden her without a saddle and without a harness or reins. He could have just sat upon her bare back and she would move with him like they were of one mind, thanks to the touch of his thighs and the subtle movements of his body—many of which he wasn't sure he was aware of.

That girl had to know him better than he knew himself.

As he opened his eyes and let go of Ginger so she could eat, he looked down on the floor of the barn. In the dirty hay outside the door of Bessie's stall was a red hair tie. He walked over and picked it up off the floor. There was a bunch of brown hair stuck around it.

He couldn't think of the last time they'd had a woman in the barn—except Emily yesterday when she had brought the horses back. Even then, he couldn't remember if she had been in the barn. Plus, she didn't seem like the red scrunchie type of girl. In fact, he'd remembered exactly the kind of black hair band he'd pulled out of her hair last night before he'd kissed her. It was the same kind she had in her hair this morning.

He dropped the hair tie back onto the ground, wishing

he hadn't picked it up. He'd made a mistake moving it from where he'd first noticed it.

It was probably nothing, he told himself as he made his way outside toward Emily and the deputy and detective who were still standing around and talking.

"Emily?" he asked, feeling strange interrupting the group.

They all went silent.

He realized his misstep as he'd called her by her first name. "I mean *Deputy Monahan*. I think I found something in the barn that might be of interest. Something that doesn't make sense." He motioned for them to follow. "It's small, but..."

They followed him inside the barn.

"I know I shouldn't have, but I picked it up to see what it was. There is brunette hair on it. I think it's a woman's hair tie. We don't have any women working on the ranch and we haven't had any women guests that I've known about in the last few weeks—at least not after the last barn cleanup. That was just last week. We had Trevor do a full muck-out."

"And you know for sure that there are no girls on his crew?" Detective Bullock asked.

He nodded.

Bullock waved over at a woman who was carrying a camera and, until now, Cameron hadn't noticed. The woman started to make her way over. "This is our evidence tech, Adrianna Walken. I'm going to have her go over the barn. We'd walked through but hadn't found anything in here that we considered to be a part of the active crime scene. Now, that is going to change. That means you will have to leave."

"I can't leave the horses uncared for." He shook his head adamantly.

Bullock crossed his arms over his chest and looked down at the floor as though he was thinking. He paused for a long moment. "I can respect that. This is a working ranch. I won't keep you out, but please don't disturb anything else before we have a chance to document everything. Fair?"

Cameron nodded. "I need to water them then I can be done for the day."

"That's not a problem."

Emily cleared her throat, getting his attention. "Didn't you need to move the cattle?"

He looked back at Ginger, who had stuck her head over the door of her stall and was looking out at them with curiosity. "I do. They need to get on fresh grass soon." He thought for a moment. "I need to get in touch with Trevor and see if he can run them without me."

"Perfect. In the meantime, we are going to get the bodies off to the medical examiner. I'm going to push to have the autopsies done quickly." Bullock looked like he wanted to add something but he remained silent. "As soon as you're done watering the horses, I'd appreciate you waiting outside the barn. Deputy Monahan will be your contact person."

Cameron nodded. Based on the look on the detective's face, he had a feeling that the man knew something less than professional had happened between him and Emily last night. Thankfully, he was discreet enough not to make a big deal about it. He could understand why Emily liked the man. Perhaps when and if they got to the bottom of this investigation, he would like the man as well.

EMILY PLACED THE black bag on the ground next to Leonard's body. The rigor had taken full effect and his corpse was totally stiff and impossible to move. She wished she could have moved him yesterday but, given the mysterious circumstances of his death and the need to fully investigate the scene, she could understand why Bullock hadn't wanted to release the bodies.

Adrianna got in close, taking pictures of the hilt of the knife. There was a bloody handprint on the elk-antler handle. It looked as though Adrianna had already gotten prints off the handle, thanks to some powder left in the creases of the horn. It was a beautiful knife.

Ruanas had a reputation of being well crafted and each one was handmade and one of a kind. They had been around for multiple generations and when she had looked this morning, some of the older knives were selling online for tens of thousands of dollars. Even the new ones weren't cheap and carried a price tag of several hundred dollars.

From what Bullock had said when he'd looked over the body—though he hadn't removed any clothing items and had done just a basic inspection—it had appeared as though Leonard had been stabbed at least ten times. Several times in the abdomen, as well as many defensive injuries to the backs of his arms.

Leaning down, she peeked at the arms of his jean jacket and looked at the bloodied edges of his sleeves. The man had definitely put up a good fight. She had to guess he was a lot like Cameron. She would think he would do just the same—except she couldn't imagine, or maybe it was *bear*, the thought of Cameron losing the battle for his life.

After making sure Adrianna had taken all the pictures she had needed of the front of the body, Emily placed a tube over the knife in the man's chest and carefully secured it in place to make sure it wouldn't be disturbed during their transit or move to the medical examiner's office.

She pulled the bag under Leonard's leg. "You ready to lift him?"

"Let's turn him to the side so I can get pictures under him and behind him on the truck," Adrianna said, pushing back the sleeves on her black office-issued jacket with big yellow letters on the front that read "Tech."

Emily stood up and checked to make sure that Cameron was out of sight.

He was sitting on the buckboard bench in front of the barn. His fingers were tented between his knees like he was deep in thought. She couldn't believe how cool, calm and collected he was in the face of his family's storm.

It struck her as odd that he could be so emotionally reserved. He was either the kind who came out of the womb with extreme serenity, or he had been a product of life beating him down to the point of emotional numbness. She hoped that he was just calm by nature.

In her work, she had come across both kinds in men and women. It seemed like the beaten-by-life types came with a look in their eyes that was unmistakable: a cloud of darkness that couldn't be lifted no matter how much laughter or joy seeped in around the edges of their agony. It was like it was a permanent storm in the center of their soul, like the storm on Saturn that would never abate and instead threatened to swallow up or destroy whatever got in its way.

She thought about the look he had given her last night; the want. He had needed her last night, but until now she thought it had been because of some ethereal connection between them. However, standing by his father's body, she wondered if perhaps it was that he'd needed to be comforted and she had simply been the closest person.

The thought tore at her in ways she couldn't deal with at the moment and she turned back to Leonard.

She motioned for Deputy Vetter to help her with the man's body. Vetter looked over at Cameron and smirked. She wanted to slap the look right off his face.

"Why don't you take the upper body?" she said, motioning toward his shoulder. "Let's tip him to the right and take some pictures and we will move the bag under. We need to make sure we get good images of everything we can before we get him out of here."

Vetter nodded. "You got it, boss."

He was pushing it. Until now, they had been getting along. She didn't know why he'd called her "boss." It wasn't like him to call her names or put her down. She had been giving him more instructions than normal though. Maybe he was just having a bad morning or something.

They walked over to the remains and Vetter pulled the body to the right. He moaned; the sound low and guttural as the corpse expelled pent-up gases. The sound made the hair on her arms rise even though she had heard it many times before.

There was no give in any of Leonard's limbs and his body was heavy with death. He lay oddly on the ground, off-center, with his head rigid and unmoving on his shoulders.

Behind the man, on the truck's fender, was a smeared bloody handprint. "Holy…" Vetter said.

"Detective!" she called to Bullock, who was talking on his phone just inside the open doors of the barn. "You need to get over here."

He rushed over, slipping the phone into his pocket.

Adrianna was clicking away with her camera and she placed an evidence tag, which included a ruler, next to the print, carefully documenting it.

From the way the handprint sat, it looked as though Leonard had grabbed the truck as he had started to fall. However, it was also possible that the handprint they were looking at wasn't his but the person's who had killed him—if they had put his body in that position.

Based on the position of Ben's body inside the house and the staging of the gun, she had to think that Leonard's body had been staged, too. It was a strange position, to make him look like he was sleeping outside against his pickup. It was almost as if the person who had killed him had wanted whoever came upon the scene not to recognize the man was dead for a while. In fact, that was exactly what had happened.

But why would someone need to do something like that? Why would they need more time?

Or maybe the person hadn't meant to kill Leonard. They had placed him in a manner that could have indicated respect. There had been a pretty significant fight. That had to mean they were likely looking for a man—someone who Leonard would have gone to in a fight. It would have had to have been someone stronger than the older rancher. But that was saying a lot.

Bullock didn't say anything, but he was taking notes in his phone. Whenever he did that, she knew to leave him alone; it meant he was in the zone. Maybe he was making more headway in the case.

According to what he'd told them when she'd arrived at the ranch, they had a positive on the smear on the hallway that it was human blood and they had managed to pull a series of fingerprints. He'd planned on having the fingerprints run through the database today. Unfortunately, the prints on the knife had come back as completely unusable thanks to the texture of the elk antler on the grip.

Maybe they could get lucky with this print. They wouldn't know if they got what they needed to identify who had been on this ranch besides the Trapper men until they were back at the office.

The sooner, the better—that way, Cameron's name could be cleared.

A thought struck her… *What if the handprint is Cameron's?*

She pushed away the intrusive thought. There was no way. "Is it okay if we continue to move him, Detective?"

Bullock looked up at her and stared for a long moment, like he needed to come back to reality before he could answer. "Sure. Let's get both bodies out of here. I think we have most of what we need. This…this might also help." He nudged his chin in the direction of the fender.

It didn't take long for her and Vetter to get the bag around the stiff body. Leonard's seated remains, complete with the knife tube sticking out of his chest, looked strange in the body bag on the gurney.

Deputy Vetter stood at the end of the gurney as they wheeled it toward the coroner's van Vetter had brought from the office on the detective's orders. Maybe that had been part of his annoyance with her, as she was the acting coroner and he had been tasked with running the bodies around in her stead since she had been asked to help with questioning Cameron.

"Can you believe this?" Vetter whispered, looking toward Cameron to make sure he couldn't hear him.

"Believe what?" she asked.

"Cameron had to have done this. He's guilty," he said,

taking her by surprise. "He stands to inherit the whole place with his dad and brother out of the way. Plus, he did one hell of a chop job pressing his dad's fingerprints on the gun before staging it in his brother's hand. That whole scene was just *bad*."

"He didn't—"

"Dollars to donuts, that handprint on the truck is Cameron's." He motioned toward the truck as they neared the black coroner's van that was parked near the eighteen-wheeler set up for moving cattle. He stared at Cameron for a long moment, as though he was weighing and measuring him with his gaze before looking back at her. "Detective Bullock's good. He's going to love to string him up by his ankles."

"Bullock won't stop until he gets blood on his teeth, that is for sure, but Cameron didn't do this. He isn't the type and there are two other sisters he would have to share his inheritance with. That doesn't quite add up." She checked her annoyance with the deputy as she opened the back doors of the van. As it opened, it smelled like stale air and death. "Ready to put him in?"

Vetter nodded.

Thankfully, even though they had an office with a limited budget, they had a lift for their gurneys, so no one ever had to haul bodies in and out of the vehicles. It had saved many people from getting hurt. After getting the body up and clicking him into place, she stepped out and closed the doors. When she turned, Cameron was staring directly at her and she caught his gaze.

"I'm going to ask him a few questions," she said to Vetter, motioning toward Cameron with her chin.

"You need backup?"

She waved off the newbie deputy who couldn't read

the get-lost vibe she was really trying to put off. "Why don't you go ahead and get started with the next body? Grab Adrianna and get the pictures done with Ben. Let me know if you need my help in there."

Though she didn't really need anything from Cameron, and she should have probably just gone inside to help with moving Ben, she couldn't stand being so close to Vetter. She could understand his line of thinking. In fact, she had thought many of the same things he had, but for some reason his assertions rubbed her all the wrong ways.

Cameron's gaze didn't waver as she sauntered over to him, swaying her hips slightly more than was necessary and, though she realized she was doing it, she didn't stop herself. It didn't make sense to her that she would allow herself to put on this little display, especially given the circumstances, but a little hint of sex couldn't make things worse for him. At least, she hoped not.

He scooted down on the bench and patted the spot beside him as she approached. "Take a seat, if you'd like." He sounded a little awkward, as though he wasn't sure he should be asking after what had happened last night and what was happening now—she didn't blame him.

She sat down beside him, spreading her legs slightly so their knees brushed against each other. He leaned in slightly instead of pulling away as she had expected. She was relieved. "How are you doing?"

"Are you actually worried about me or are you trying to just start a conversation so you can ask me more questions?" he asked, quirking an eyebrow. "If you are worried, you don't need to be and, as for interrogating me—you can just jump right to it. I have nothing to hide, and you know it."

"I know you don't. And I hope you know that I'm not

looking in your direction," she countered, trying to not find his devilish charm more enticing than she should.

"Is that right?" He gave her a rakish smile that made whatever reticence she had in falling for this man slip away. She couldn't help herself; he was the sexiest cowboy she had ever seen and, dammit, if he didn't know.

"Did you talk to your ranch hand?" she asked.

"Trevor?"

She nodded.

"I've been texting him, letting him know what has been happening on the ranch. He hasn't said much, which isn't outside the norm. This morning, he hasn't been responding at all. Which also isn't unlike him. When he gets like this, I just GPS his ass. Today, I tracked his location to The Mint Bar downtown. I'll have to run down there to talk to him. You game?"

She nodded. "For now, we are at a standstill while Bullock is going through the barn. The bodies need to get to the ME, and we are waiting on results from the fingerprints. Since he lives on the ranch, we do need to get a statement from him."

"I can't promise he is sober."

"Was he on the ranch in the last two days?"

Cam shook his head. "I don't think so. He was supposed to be with his kid."

That was one dead-end lead, but she'd still need Trevor's statement.

She couldn't stop staring at Cam and a smile flickered over her lips. It took her by surprise, given the circumstances, but she couldn't help herself.

With him looking at her like that, she wished things could have continued last night. There were storm clouds within his eyes, but when he looked at her, the storm seemed to calm, and the tempest within her did the same.

She took in a breath as she recalled the way his hand had moved up the back of her neck and through her hair. It was so intense, the way he had touched her. He had taken her like he had owned her. There was no being timid or questions—only possession.

Chapter Ten

It took longer than expected to leave the ranch. Emily ended up having to help the young-looking deputy load up Ben's body into the back of the black coroner's van.

It was strange sitting there watching his family disappear into the vehicle. It didn't escape him that it was quite possibly the last time he would see them.

His family wasn't the kind to do a big wake or viewing, but after the cremations, perhaps he would have Reverend Daniels come over to the ranch and do a little service for family friends. He'd have to order a headstone for the family plot. He wasn't even sure if there was a place in the graveyard for his brother. He only knew there was one for his father because when his mother had died, they had both put their names on the headstone together. All he had to do was add the date.

It was also strange, and so surreal. It wasn't that he hadn't thought about his father's potential demise, it was just that he had never expected it to come so soon or unexpectedly. Like most of the men in his family, he thought his father would live into his mideighties and go out strong. Though, from what Emily had said, he had gone out as a fighter.

It felt strange being back in the passenger seat of the

squad car again, and perhaps that was adding to his feelings. In some ways it all felt unavoidable—like death and taxes. He chuckled, the sound under his breath.

At least he was in the front of the car and his wrists weren't in cuffs. His mom would never have believed such a thing when he was younger. He and Ben had been wild children growing up—throwing bottle rockets down the culverts and whipping snowballs at passing cars on the highways. More than once, they'd had the police show up on their doorstep.

The Mint Bar was at the opposite end of West Glacier from Emily's place, but not too far from the ranch. It harkened back to days when the ranch hands would get off work and pile into pickups and head down to the watering hole and then stagger back to the ranch at the end of the night. Based on the aesthetic of the place, not much had changed from those days, either.

It was a dive by anyone's standards. The flickering neon lights in the windows and the faded band posters kept most of the nonlocals at bay as most tourists who came to West Glacier were looking for the glitz and glam of the Montana experience that they saw on television, not the true state that was built on cow patties and wheat hulls.

Where there was that type of required labor, there was also a different culture that came with it that few talked about—the low-rent bordellos and brothels that had once been scattered up and down the streets of every town in the West. That wasn't to say those kinds of services weren't still available. From what he'd heard from Ben and the boys around the ranch, they certainly were, but they were no longer nearly as obvious or as advertised.

As he walked with Emily up to the front door of The Mint, he looked up to the second floor of the Old West–

style brick-and-white-stucco building. There were six small windows and they were set closely together. The rooms upstairs must have been small—the kind that were used for the specialty services offered by the soiled doves.

The bells on the door jingled as they made their way inside the bar. It smelled like stale beer, fryer grease, and decades of cigarettes even though smoking was no longer allowed in public buildings. The floor was sticky as they made their way up to the bar where there were five men already seated and drinking mugs of pilsners. It reminded him of growing up as he had spent more nights in here playing darts and drinking beer with Ben and his friends than he could even remember.

The thought of those nights made a piercing pain stab through his chest. He was going to miss his brother. They had been best friends for the better parts of their lives.

Sure, they had gone their separate ways in the recent past. But there had been a part of him that had held out a hope that one day his brother would come home and they would go back to the old days—when they'd been tight. Things would never have been the same, but they could have learned to like each other again.

He would never forget the time his brother had found a deceased skunk and had been told to move it away from the house. Instead of carefully moving it without touching the animal, the kid had pushed it onto a shovel with his cowboy boot. Later that night, he'd worn his boots into the house and put them in front of the air intake for the entire house.

Their mother had been furious.

He'd spent hours scrubbing those boots—and making it up to their mom.

It had taken weeks for the smell to completely disappear from the house.

Emily paused and looked over at him. She'd pulled her hair loose, letting it fall over her shoulders. He loved that look on her, it made her appear less rigid and more approachable, and perhaps that was why she had chosen to do it. "Which one is your hand?" she whispered, glancing in the direction of the bar.

She looked so beautiful in her uniform with her hair down that he felt a niggle of covetousness within him. He wanted to tell all the men in the bar that she was his. He'd never felt that way in his life, but everything about her and what was happening between them was different than anything that he'd felt before.

Besides, she wasn't his and he wasn't hers. They had kissed, nothing more.

When had he become a guy who took a kiss so seriously? He had been going through so much. Maybe she had just taken pity on him and wanted to make him feel better. Though the detective she worked with hadn't said anything about him calling her by her first name, he could tell that she was probably going to hear about that later. And he didn't want to be the reason she got in trouble at work. He wasn't worth the risk. He was just a dumb ranch kid with more trouble on his plate than reward he could offer.

"He's the one at the end there," he said, pointing in Trevor's direction. "Give me a minute and I will talk to him. He may not respond well to a deputy rolling up on him if he has been drinking."

Trevor had been known to have a temper on bad days—at least when he'd been young and dumb. Cameron would like to assume he'd outgrown his temper, but when it came to Emily, he wasn't about to take any chances.

Trevor was talking to the guy next to him and didn't seem to have noticed them. Cam made his way over and as he neared, Trevor finally looked up and saw him. His eyes were red from a long night—or days—of drinking and little to no sleep. To say he looked rough was an understatement. In fact, he wasn't sure that he had ever seen Trevor look this bad.

"How you doing, man?" he asked, moving to the bar next to the ranch hand.

Trevor was wearing a hat that had once been light brown but now was nearly black thanks to sweat, dirt and time. He was wearing a loose-fitting, button-down Ariat shirt that had worn out around the corners of the breast pockets to the point you could see the once-white tank top he wore beneath. He smelled like piss and Copenhagen. He was in a rough way and if Cam had to guess, it had been more than just a couple of days since he'd taken a shower.

Trevor grunted, looking down at the beer in his hand. "I've had better damned days, but I got no right complainin' to you." He lifted the beer and took a long, drawn-out slug. He slammed the glass down on the bar after draining the rest of the liquid and motioned for the bartender to get him another.

She gave Cameron a questioning look and he shook his head, letting her know he wasn't interested in drinking this early.

The bartender wiped her hands on the rag at her waist before making her way over and grabbing Trevor's mug to pour him another. They sat in silence watching her work until she returned with a foamy beer. "You sure you don't want anything?" She looked over at Emily. "Whatever she and you want…it's on the house."

"Thanks, but she's on the clock and it's a little early for me."

"This is the guy I was telling you about," Trevor said to the bartender.

She looked at him and her eyes widened. "Oh, man, I'm so sorry to hear about your dad and your brother." She wiped her hands on the towel again, like it was a safety blanket. "I met your brother just the other night. He was a decent guy. Tipped me well."

"What?" he asked, taken aback. "You met Ben?"

The bartender nodded, but another couple had walked in and she was called away to the other end of the bar where they had sat down and were ready to order drinks. Cameron motioned for Emily to come over. "Trev, I want you to meet the deputy that is helping investigate our case. This is Deputy Monahan. She's doing one heck of a job."

Trevor stood up and moved to make room for her to take his spot at the bar. "Nice to meet you, Deputy," he said, giving her an acknowledging tip of the head. "I appreciate all you're doin' to help out the ranch. It's gonna be real tough on all of us. Hell, it already is."

"I'm sorry for your losses, Trevor." Emily put her hand on his shoulder and Trevor twitched slightly as he leaned into the bar.

He sloppily moved out of her touch and sat on a barstool farther down the bar. "Let me get you guys some lunch," he said, motioning for them both to sit. "They do actually have pretty good burgers here, and I could probably use a bite. That is, if they are serving food. We may have to ask, it's a little early." His words came slow, like he was forcing them through the hazy fog of alcohol.

The fact that he could be so coherent given how he

smelled and looked was impressive. That, or he hadn't been drinking as long or as hard as Cameron had assumed.

Emily sent him a glance that told him she could use some food and conversation. He was glad she was up to being a good sport around a bad drunk.

Cameron sat down beside Trevor. "Did you know that the bartender—"

"Heidi." Trevor pointed a finger at the blonde pouring two drafts.

"Yes, Heidi," Cameron said, continuing. "Did you know she had seen Ben?"

He shrugged. "She mentioned it, but we didn't talk about it much. Didn't seem real important. Everyone stops by the bar on their way into town, you know how it is. It's the best way to get in touch with your friends. You know everyone's here."

He wasn't wrong, at least not when it came to the group of friends Ben ran with. The same couldn't be said of Cameron's, at least not anymore. Though he couldn't say he had very many friends beyond the feed store people, the diner staff and other ranchers.

A man a few barstools down from them stood up. He was wearing a green vest over a blue-flannel shirt. His hair was long, and he wore it pulled back into a ponytail that spilled down his back. Cameron didn't know why, but the guy seemed out of place in the bar and, as he looked at him, he quickly threw money on the bar and hightailed it outside. Strange.

"You know that guy?" he asked Trevor, motioning after the dude who'd just left.

Trevor shook his head. "He's been sitting there for a bit. Didn't say much. Just that he's from North Dakota. Traveling through."

"North Dakota?" Emily asked, leaning over the bar so she could look directly at Trevor.

"Yeah, why?" He gave a one-shoulder shrug.

"That's where Ben was coming from, right?" she asked.

"Yeah," Cam said, nodding.

It was a long haul from North Dakota to West Glacier and there wasn't a direct route. For someone to want to get from one place to the other, they had to connect from a variety of highways and onto and off Interstate 90. They'd have to *want* to get to West Glacier—it was just a dot on a map if someone wasn't headed to Glacier National Park. No one was just *traveling through* from North Dakota. His statement didn't pass the sniff test.

Cameron gave Emily an appraising glance and she shot him a rise of the brows. She must have been thinking along the same lines.

Heidi came sauntering back over, towel in hand. "Did I hear you guys say you wanted to order some food?"

"Get 'em a couple of cheeseburgers, fries and all the fixin's," Trevor ordered, not waiting for a menu or for them to make any decisions.

It didn't matter to Cam, but he wasn't sure about Emily. He checked, but instead of seeming annoyed or put out, Emily just nodded at the bartender. "After you let the cook know our order, would you mind coming back though? I need to ask you a few more questions about Ben."

Heidi glanced down the bar and, making sure everyone had full beers, she nodded. "I'll be right back."

Trevor took another long drink of his beer. "I saw you called. I'm sorry I didn't answer, Cam."

Cameron tipped his head. "It's okay. I get it. I'm having a hard time with everything as well. However, you know that we have to get back to work. Things are still needing to get done back at the WGC."

Trevor didn't say anything, and his head just dropped low over his beer as he nodded. "I know we gotta finish moving the cattle up to the mountain—that's overdue. I just… Your dad is normally the one who heads that up."

He and Cam's father were extremely close, as Trevor had nearly grown up on the ranch. He'd worked there since he was eighteen years old and had lived down in the bunkhouse near the stock pond after he had come to the ranch when his parents had kicked him out. He hadn't graduated from high school and his prospects in life hadn't been great, but he'd always had an incredibly strong work ethic. In fact, the ranch was the one thing he cared about above anything else.

The only problems they'd ever had with him were a few trips to the drunk tank and a fistfight that had ended in a broken beer bottle to the side of his head, which had nearly taken off his ear. They had ended up taking him into the emergency room and sitting with him while he'd gotten nearly one hundred stitches. The doc had told him he needed to go to a plastic surgeon but, of course, the cowboy had told him he didn't need to look pretty—he just needed to have an ear attached to his head.

"I know you loved my dad. We all did…at least most of the time," Cameron said with a laugh as he thought about all the times he had lost his patience with his dad. He'd even been angry with Leonard yesterday when he'd arrived on the ranch about the financial state of the place.

What a confusing mess that was turning out to be, thanks to the banking records they had gone through last night.

Cam wouldn't be surprised if it took months for the

detective to get to the bottom of what had happened with his father and brother—that was, if he was ever able to make sense of the mess things had become. He was certainly at a loss.

"Your dad did more for me than any other person on this planet. I wouldn't have had a home if it hadn't been for him." Trevor's voice cracked as he spoke, and it made Cameron pause.

He hadn't realized until now why Trevor would have been so upset. Of course, he not only would have been saddened by the family's loss, but he would also be afraid that he was no longer going to be a part of the ranch.

"Trevor, just so you know, as long as I'm on the ranch, you will be, too." Cameron put his hand on the guy's shoulder. "Now that Ben's gone, you are the closest person I have left to a brother. I'm going to need your help more than ever."

Trevor perked up. He lifted his head and some of the heaviness that had been in his eyes seemed to dissipate. "You don't have to say that just to make me feel better. I don't need pity."

"You know I don't do pity."

Trevor looked at Emily.

"Not even to get a lady," Cameron added, smirking at Trevor.

"You read my damned mind." Trevor finally smiled.

Heidi walked over. "Did you say something about a lady?"

Cameron winked at Trevor. "I can't say the same thing about you when it comes to getting ladies," he leaned in and whispered.

Trevor smirked.

Emily smiled at Heidi. "We were talking about you,"

she fibbed. "You said you had seen Ben in here. When was that, exactly?"

"He was in here twice actually. But the first night it was just really quick with some woman." Heidi looked up and to the left, like she was trying to recall a memory. "She was dark-haired, thin and looked worse for the wear, if you know what I mean."

Emily nodded. "Did you know this woman?"

Heidi shook her head. "I hadn't seen her around here before. Ben didn't introduce her, and though they had come in together, they left separately. I didn't see who she left with though. All I know is that she was gone when he decided to go."

"And you didn't see her come in with him the following night?" Emily asked.

Heidi shook her head. "The next night he was in here and he was chatting with the guy who just left." She took a couple steps down the bar and picked up the cash the guy had left and tapped it on the wood before turning and closing out his bill. She stuffed the couple of ones left over in the silver canister next to the till. "He was just as cheap with his tips as he was the other night, too."

"Do you know him? Is he a regular?"

Again, Heidi shook her head. "He has only been coming in this last week or so. Doesn't really talk much. Gotta say, it's kind of nice, but it's unusual for someone who takes a seat at the bar. Usually when someone sits up here, it means they are looking to talk to me—either to share a sob story or to chat me up. He didn't seem interested in either."

Cam'd never thought about the sociology of a bar before and why people picked where they sat, but the bartender was probably right. When he didn't want to talk to people, he sat away from the bar at a table and pretended to watch sports on the big screen. He would walk up to the bar to get a drink when he wanted one, or he would wait for the server to wait on him. And, if he really didn't want to talk, he wouldn't have been in the bar in the first place.

It made him wonder why the man had come there.

When he had heard who they were, and the conversations they were having, he hadn't even taken the time to get his check or finish his beer. He had been in one hell of a hurry to leave.

"Do you know where we could possibly find that guy?" he asked.

Heidi shrugged. "Like I said, he didn't really talk to me."

Trevor shot him a sideways glance as Emily said something he couldn't quite hear to the bartender. He watched as she slipped the girl her business card.

Trevor knew something and, for the first time since he'd realized his father was dead, Cam finally felt like he was getting close to finding answers.

Chapter Eleven

It was clear Trevor was in no shape to take the cattle up on the mountain or give a statement that was usable in court. Cameron and Emily ate their lunch, paid the tab and made their way out of the bar.

The burgers had been just as good as Trevor had promised. Her stomach was full, and they had spent the last hour talking about Trevor and Cameron growing up on the ranch.

She'd had no idea that they had spent so much time together. They'd seemed just as close as Cameron and Ben in many ways. In fact, maybe closer. It was no wonder that Trevor had found his way to the bar while everything was happening at the ranch. If she had had a choice to stay or leave in a situation like theirs, she would have gone to the bar as well.

She sent a quick text message to her neighbor to check on Stacy. Penny messaged a second later and said she was doing great.

Emily got in the cruiser and tapped her fingers on the steering wheel, humming away.

Her phone pinged with messages from Bullock. He'd been busy all morning. They hadn't found much in the barn, but there had been some footprints that seemed consistent with women's cowboy boots. He was going to look into it a little further, along with Adrianna and Vetter.

According to Bullock, the bodies had been delivered to the crime lab in Missoula and they would try to get the results back to them as quickly as possible. Depending on the backlog of cases, that could mean anywhere from half a day to two weeks.

Going to the bar had been far more helpful than she could have ever expected or anticipated—even without getting an official statement from Trevor. It was funny how things worked out sometimes.

This wasn't the first time in her career where she had just gotten lucky and been in the right place at the right time. That was actually how she had become a cop in the first place.

She hadn't grown up dreaming about being a police officer. No, far from it.

Emily had always thought she would go into something with animals. She had always had an affinity for stray cats, adopting them off the streets then bringing them home, cleaning them up, feeding them and nursing them back to health. Most of the times, they would disappear the next day—probably to go back to their real house—but she had always felt like she was saving the world one kitty at a time.

Her life would have been so different if she'd become a vet. She looked over at Cameron. He was texting away on his phone and he seemed to be deep in thought.

Since they had left the bar, he had been acting a little bit strange. From the atmosphere between Trevor and Cameron, it was like there had been a conversation bonding them that she wasn't privy to, and she didn't like it. She wanted to ask what was going on or what had happened, but she decided to just wait to see if Cameron would open up to her.

"Did you find anything out from the bartender about the guy?" Cameron asked.

"Just what you heard. I gave her my card and made sure she knew that she could call me if he returned to the bar. He definitely seemed in a hurry to get out of there when he saw us. Had you ever seen that guy before?"

Cameron shook his head. "I wonder if we looked up my brother's phone records if we could see if he was calling somebody else here in town. That might link us up with this guy."

She texted detective Bullock about the records. "Done. Good idea. We'll see if we can come up with anything, but sometimes getting those records takes a little bit."

"You know, I thought this detective thing worked a whole lot faster." Cameron turned slightly in his seat as he looked at her.

She laughed. "Dude, real police work isn't anything like TV. Even the initial investigation takes forever. At least, it feels like it. Sometimes it can take a couple of weeks before we even release the initial crime scene. Though, I think we'll be done with the one at the ranch within the next day or so."

He seemed surprised. "I seriously thought it would take like a day and we could get right back in. In fact, I thought I'd be sleeping in my own bed tonight. You're saying I won't be?"

She shook her head. "I highly doubt it. I'm sorry to tell you that."

As soon as she said that, she was tempted to invite him to come back to her place and spend the night once again. On the other hand, she was worried about Stacy and what she would think. It was strange enough for Emily to have a man spend the night once, but what would her daughter think of him spending twice in a row? She didn't want Stacy to get too emotionally connected to this guy when he was nothing more than a part of a case—even if he had kissed her.

To mask her confusion, she put the car in gear and pulled out of the bar parking lot. She didn't know where she was going. The next logical step would have been to track down the man who had last been seen with Ben, but she had no idea where to start looking.

She started to head aimlessly toward Main Street, but turned left so she wouldn't have to drive past the diner and the alley that led to her house. She didn't want either of them getting any ideas.

If she really thought about it, the person she was most worried about getting attached to Cameron was herself. She couldn't have him spend another night if she was going to keep him at arm's length. If he kissed her again like he did before, she would never be able to remain objective with him. As it was, there was no forgetting how he had felt against her skin.

Just the thought of him kissing her made her want to drive him straight back to her place. She shifted in her seat at the thought.

As though he could read her mind, Cameron reached over and took her hand with his. He did it with authority and ownership, but it was also considerate and gentle— as if she had a choice to retract her hand but he already knew she wouldn't.

He squeezed her hand tightly when she didn't pull away. She smiled over at him. "I don't know what we're doing," she said, "and I don't want to analyze it. Are you okay if this is all it is, at least for now?"

"I don't want to put you in a compromising position with your job or your investigation. I get that this," he said, motioning to each of them with his free hand, "is probably because you feel sorry for me and you're trying to comfort me, or something. But whatever it is, I'm grateful. I'm glad to have you in my corner. I'm glad to have your hand in mine." He lifted her hand up and kissed the back of it softly. "And yes, I'm totally fine with this being all we are."

"Thank you."

"And for tonight," he continued, "why don't you take me to the Arrow Lodge at the edge of town and just drop me off? They take cash and they are cheap. It's all I need for one night."

She nodded.

She couldn't believe how self-aware this cowboy was. Most cowboys she'd met couldn't put sentences together that were more than four words. He constantly impressed her. Yet she kept pushing him away. She wanted to tell him that she wanted more and that she wanted him to come home with her and that she wanted a relationship. She wanted somebody to help her raise Stacy. However, she also didn't want to force that role onto any man.

She wanted to have a relationship that worked first, not a dad for Stacy and then a relationship. Far too many of her recently divorced friends with young kids had made that exact mistake. They had fallen for men who had befriended their child or children simply because their children liked the guy. They'd forgotten about the fact that first they had to have aligning values and attractions to the actual man.

While Emily knew there was no question that she was incredibly attracted to Cameron—the instant she had seen him on the ranch she had thought he was quite possibly the sexiest man she had ever seen, complete with the cowboy hat—she couldn't say she knew everything about him. The bar had proven that.

It had also demonstrated that there was so much more to him that she enjoyed. Just now, he'd proven to her that he knew who he was and that he was in touch with what he wanted and that he could vocalize his needs. That in and of itself was strange for any man. At least, any man she had ever dated in the past. Maybe he was just too good for her.

What if he was out of her league?

"You know, you're worried that I'm just being nice to you because I'm trying to make you feel better. However, how do I know that you're not doing the same thing with me?" She turned the squad car toward the highway. "Maybe you felt bad for me after you watched me be humiliated by my ex-husband."

"You guys were something," Cam said, whistling through his teeth.

"We did put on quite a show, but that was nothing. He's done so much worse to me, I almost hate to admit it to you." She ran her hand over her face as she groaned. "I just need to shut up. I shouldn't be telling you."

"Stop. You don't need to worry. I told you. I know how exes can be. I have an ex-wife, too, April. We went through some pretty tough days."

"You didn't tell me why you guys broke up. What happened?" she asked.

Now he was the one who appeared to be shifting uncomfortably in his seat, but it seemed to be for entirely different reasons. "I was away from the ranch a lot. At least, the ranch house. It was my job at the time to go to a lot of the sales. I also did a lot of work in Helena to lobby for agricultural stipends and learn how we could best manage our finances according to state law."

Now his self-awareness and articulation made more sense. He wasn't just a cowboy; he was also a statesman and a politician. Though, who wasn't to say a cowboy couldn't be self-aware, even if she hadn't met one.

"I hope you know you're getting sexier by the minute." She smiled at him. "But continue your story."

He chuckled, but there was a tiredness in his voice that told her there was a lot of pain behind what had happened with his ex-wife. "While I was gone, it was a known fact that my wife wasn't happy. I knew it as well."

She had a sinking feeling that she knew where this story was headed, and as much as she didn't want him to have to continue, she needed to know for sure.

"If I had been older and wiser, I would have come home and taken her right into my arms and had her travel all over the state with me. I would have made us go into marriage counseling or whatever needed to be done. However, I was stupid. I thought things could be handled over the phone and through texting. When I called, she said she was fine. I believed her. I mean we didn't fight."

She felt for him. "How did you guys meet?"

"She and I went to high school together. It was stupid. We were the yearbook couple, if you know what I mean. Homecoming queen and king. Voted the couple that was most likely to get married. It was funny, though, because in reality we weren't having sex and we weren't doing the things that people assumed we were. In high school, we were mostly just really good friends, and we watched movies together and just hung out like buddies."

She nodded. "I had really great friends that were of the

opposite sex as well. Nobody gets it. Everyone always assumes that there is some romantic element."

He pinched his lips together as he nodded. "Yeah. And we tried to navigate that," he said, moving his hand like it was a raft navigating a turbulent river. "However we ended up just giving in to what everybody assumed. And we were stuck in this relationship and stuck into marriage because it was the logical next step. And we loved each other enough. I thought that we made each other happy."

Reminded of her thoughts on true love from just yesterday. "Do you believe in true love?"

He made a strange, strangling noise. "Can you define that for me?" he asked after a long pause.

Once again, she was taken aback by how much they had in common. However, this time she wasn't sure that she entirely liked it. Part of her wished that he knew the answer and he would sweep her away with some grand rejoinder about love. Maybe she was totally warped by romantic movies just like he was about cop shows. They both had assumed some things and gotten them completely wrong.

The hotel he wanted her to take him to wasn't far down the road. It was a little bit too early for check-in, but in a place like this, normally they would sign him in no matter what time. However, she didn't want to have him leave her just yet, so she slowed way down. Cars started passing them on the highway, even though she was in her police unit. Normally, it would have annoyed her, but today she didn't even give it a second thought. Instead, all she could think about was love.

"If I could define true love for you, I don't think I'd be divorced. In fact, I don't think I would have been married in the first place. That being said, I don't have any regrets. Like every parent before me that's gone through divorce and has a child, I'm really grateful that I have my daughter. I wouldn't be the same without her—she's the reason I'm alive."

He quirked his eyebrow. "See, I'm glad I didn't have kids because I don't think I could have left. Even with the circumstances being what they were."

"You didn't tell me what happened…"

He sighed, the sound filled the space between them and, even though it was quiet in that moment, it sounded louder than the highway noise under their tires. "When I came home from my last trip to Helena, I walked into the bunkhouse where she and I lived, and she was in there with Ben."

She thought that his sigh had been loud, but her gasp was ten times louder.

Of all the things she thought he was going to tell her, that had been near the bottom of the list. However, his re-action to his father's and brother's deaths did make a hell of a lot more sense now. It was no wonder that he hadn't cried. He had to have been experiencing so many emo-tions; emotions that she hadn't even started to understand yesterday.

Even now, knowing what she did, she couldn't under-stand how this man was functioning.

They drove in silence all the way to the hotel. She had no idea what to say.

She wanted to thank him for being honest and telling her what had to be his most embarrassing and raw secret. It had to be humiliating to admit that his brother had done him so wrong. He had spoken about Ben being his best friend and his comrade growing up. For his brother to have done something so brutal with a woman he'd also grown up with had to be so painful.

She wanted to just take him in her arms and hold him and make everything right. But how could a man like him, who had been through so much betrayal, ever trust anyone, let alone a virtual stranger like her. People he had known for years had lied to him. Who was to say that she wouldn't?

How had he even been strong enough to want to kiss her? He'd had to make himself so vulnerable to want to do something like that with her.

It had meant so much last night for him to take that step, but now that single kiss meant even more.

She hated it.

They had promised each other that their holding hands would be as far as this would go today. For this horribly broken man, she now realized that promises were something that couldn't be broken.

Chapter Twelve

Cameron looked at the seedy '70s era hotel and settled deeper into the front seat of Emily's car. She hadn't argued when he'd asked her to bring him here, but he'd wished she would have. Sure, it was logical that he wouldn't go back to her place and there was no way in hell he was going to spend a night in that bunkhouse on the ranch, but sitting here, he would have taken just about anywhere else.

"You know...that guy from the bar, he must be staying somewhere. Did you see what kind of vehicle he drove away in when he left The Mint?" he asked, stalling.

"I was thinking about that earlier," she said after a long pause.

Ever since he had opened up to her about his ex, she had been *off.* She had said that she shouldn't have told him so much about Todd, but looking at their conversation and how it turned out, he was the one who had taken things way too far.

They didn't know each other well enough for him to unleash his past onto her like he had—even if she was investigating his brother's death. What Ben had done to him several years ago had no relevance on his brother's demise.

"If you want, we can sit here for a few minutes. Do a little stakeout," he offered.

She smirked. "A stakeout?" She giggled. "Who are we, Starsky and Hutch?"

He laughed, acting put out. "Well, when you say it like that, we sound ridiculous. All I mean is that if we sit here, maybe we can catch sight of the guy."

"I like your thinking, but this isn't the 1970s and we probably aren't going to get as lucky as we did by running into him at the bar. That was just good fortune. Now he knows we might be looking for him. He will probably be laying low. Which means he isn't going to be walking out in front of black-and-whites." She motioned to her car.

"Oh," he said, feeling rejected and silly. "I'm sure you have other cases to work on. I'll let you get back to your job." He put his hand on the door handle.

He couldn't believe how selfish and wrapped up he'd gotten in his own world. Of course she had other calls and other people in the community to help. He had been so focused on his family and his past, he hadn't even stopped to consider that there might be other families out there in West Glacier who were going through their own emergencies and needed her.

"Stop." She took his hand and moved it over toward her chest and as she did, he brushed against the gun in her bellyband. "I didn't mean it like that. And I don't want you to go into this hotel, either. In fact, if we are being honest, I don't really know what I want other than for you not to go in there and I don't want to go back to working alone."

"Are you saying you don't want to be without me?" he teased.

She smiled, letting his hand fall from her chest. "Well, now I wouldn't mind quite as much."

"Ha!" He laughed. "You know you love every second." As he said it, a warmth rose in his cheeks. He hadn't meant *love*, but there was no pulling in the word after it had left his lips.

Her hand stiffened and there was a long awkward pause between them. He stared out the windshield as a woman in a pair of cut-off jeans and a hot-pink tank top walked out of one of the rooms at the far end and lit a cigarette. She leaned against the wall and perched her black boot against the rock wall behind her.

A minute later, an older man—who was probably in his late forties—came out. He was buttoning the top button of his gray short-sleeved shirt. He was wearing black Dockers and he looked like he held a white-collar job. If Cameron had to guess, he was probably a real-estate agent or something along those lines.

The guy was out of place. He was also taking a room at the hotel—though, he had a feeling he was getting the room for a different reason.

The woman took a long drag on her cigarette, tilting her head back until her blond hair that was flipped up into a claw clip actually brushed the wall behind her. She let out a cloud of smoke above her and then looked down and smiled at the man. She said something and blew the man a kiss before he turned and walked toward his newer-model Porsche that was parked a few down from them.

He stopped and his eyes widened as he spotted their car. Then he dropped his head and stared at the ground before nearly running to his car. He got in and squealed his tires as he sped away.

"Boy, that guy was in one heck of a hurry," he said.

"What he was up to can be charged as a felony in Montana. He was smart to be in a hurry—though he would have been smarter to not pay for adult pleasures in the first place."

"Is that really what you think he was doing?" he asked, actually a little surprised. Sure, he had assumed that might have been what was happening based on the location and everything, but it was one thing for him to assume and another for a cop to actually confirm his suspicions.

"It's hard to prove. The women who are involved in that type of work aren't going to admit it and they aren't going to testify. If they get arrested and they say anything, they are only charged with misdemeanors. When they get out—if they have said anything, they are beaten by their pimps...or worse."

He stared at the woman who was still smoking against the wall. She looked tired and thin. There was a large black tattoo of a phoenix on her thigh, but instead of rising from the ashes it looked as though it was rising up from the crook of her knee and going straight back into the shadows cast by her shorts.

"How do you slow this problem down?" he asked.

She gave a dry laugh. "There's no slowing down the world's oldest profession. The state has done a lot of different things to try to control it. However, there is no stopping it. From time to time, we work with the FBI and create task forces in which we run sting operations where we try to capture predators who are preying on young girls. However, beyond that, the best we can do is arrest the men who are known to buy the services."

"So, you only arrest the johns?"

"Pretty much," she said, nodding. "And we try to stop human trafficking—but mostly when it comes to young girls. Women who have been at it very long are normally enlisted by pimps. Very few are on their own for a variety of reasons. But regardless of who they work for...like

I said, they aren't going to testify against anyone who is working on the streets. It goes against their codes."

It felt a little weird to him that in their line of work, there was a code. Yet, who was he to judge.

Where he could safely make a judgment call without feeling too bad, however, was in the fact that he was not about to spend the night at that location. "On that note, I don't think I'm going to check in. I'll just go ahead and camp out tonight. It's warm enough out, the stars can be my blanket."

She let go of his hand and turned to her computer installed on the mount between them. She tapped away on the keyboard. "I put a BOLO out on a man matching the description of the guy we saw at the bar. Perhaps we can get the name. In the meantime, I'm gonna give Heidi a call and see if I can obtain video surveillance from the bar to see if I can pull his face. Maybe we can get a positive identification on him. One way or another, we need to get his name."

"You know, while you were busy with the bartender, Trevor and I got to talking," Cameron said. "Apparently, he overheard the guy we've been looking for talking a little bit. I don't know if it can help, but he said that it didn't sound like the guy knew his way around town very well."

Emily frowned. "That's not that odd if a guy said he was just passing through."

"I know, but from the way Trevor was talking about it, it kind of sounded like the guy wasn't driving. He didn't know for sure, but he thought maybe Ben had brought him here and now the guy was stranded."

Her eyebrows popped up. "And you are just now telling me this?"

"Trevor wasn't sure. And hell, we don't even know who

the guy is. It's all a guessing game. I didn't want to make things even more of a crapshoot. You know?"

She sighed. "I can appreciate the sentiment. You have to understand, though, a lot of what we do is follow dead-end leads. Sometimes we have to play Telephone, where we hear things third-hand and have to track down the truth from a variety of sources. It can be a huge undertaking."

"I figured as much. I didn't want to make things worse." And right now, as hard as they were trying, it felt like they had taken two steps forward in the investigation and then three steps back. He was even more at a loss than before. At least before, he had thought it was maybe just a murder-suicide.

Now, he knew it wasn't and he knew there were more people involved—quite possibly the man at the bar. Yet, even that was not certain.

"If the guy's stranded and he isn't driving around, then he is going to have to come back to the bar, or somewhere close to there to eat dinner. He hasn't gone too far," Emily said like she was thinking out loud rather than really talking to him. "I think we should head back into town. Maybe your stakeout idea wasn't too bad after all."

The woman leaning on the wall finally seemed to notice them. She stared over in their direction. She was squinting hard even though it wasn't that sunny. Her dark makeup was smeared down her face in places. He hadn't noticed that before, but then again, she hadn't really been looking at them. There was something in her face and the way she moved that made him wonder if she was high.

As she pushed herself off the wall with her foot, she struggled to find her balance before turning away from them. She looked over her bony shoulder at the patrol car one last time before disappearing back into the hotel room. The door slammed shut behind her.

"Is there some way we can help her?" he asked, motioning toward the closed door.

She flipped down her visor and pulled out a business card from a cardholder stacked with a variety of cards in a variety of colors. She handed him one that said, "National Human Trafficking Hotline." There was an 800 number and a tagline that read, "We'll Listen. We'll Help."

"I have found that usually working girls don't want help, or they are so abused and groomed that they don't think they deserve it. Many are ashamed and don't think their families will take them back. However, this hotline can help get them out of this lifestyle." She handed him the card.

He took it and stared down at the embossed number. He wondered how many women had stared at the number like he was now.

"You can slip it under her door—I'll keep my distance because I'm in uniform and she might freak out if she sees me approach."

He nodded as he opened the car door and stepped out into the parking lot. He moved fast, flipping the card between his fingers and making a thrumming sound as he hurried to the room. He slipped the card under the door and knocked.

He didn't wait for the woman to answer and instead jogged back to Emily.

Jumping into the squad car, he slammed the door and clicked his seat belt into place just as the woman opened the hotel room door. She looked around outside, almost as if she were expecting to see someone, and was annoyed that no one was there. Then she noticed the card on the floor.

She bent over to pick it up.

After staring at it for a long minute, she looked over at them and, in one smooth and well-practiced motion, tore the business card in two. She threw it outside and flipped them the bird before disappearing inside her room.

Emily had been right. Sometimes it was impossible to save those who weren't ready to be saved. Grooming could build a nearly impenetrable cage.

Chapter Thirteen

Emily's phone rang as they were headed back to the center of West Glacier. It was the owner of The Mint Bar, Tim Porter. She had talked with him over the years for a variety of a cases, as it wasn't uncommon for her regulars to show up or frequent local bars.

The good news was that she had a pretty good working relationship with the man. "Hey, Tim, how's it going?" she answered.

"Heya, Deputy Monahan, I heard you needed access to our camera files."

She was waiting for him to drop the bomb that she was going to need a search warrant.

While she and Tim got along, he was also the kind of bar owner who stood up for his customers. He had to walk a very fine line when it came to the small local community. He couldn't be seen by the rebels and outliers as someone who buddied up with law enforcement, but he also didn't want to screw things up with cops in case things went sideways at night and he needed to call them to help.

"I don't need everything. I was just hoping to get a good still of the bar when we were in there. If you've got one of the man who left, and of him getting into a vehicle, that would be great as well."

Tim chuckled. "Heidi already gave me a heads-up. I pulled a picture of you guys at the bar. I'll send it right over. I have watched the cameras outside. Doesn't look like the guy got into a vehicle. He walked south on Main Street, toward St. Paul's Church and the post office. You might be able to get more footage from them if you need it."

Tim was all over it. This guy definitely wasn't a regular and it was working in her favor.

"That would be great. I appreciate all your help with this, Tim. Please let me know if there's anything you need in return," she said more out of habit than anything else.

Tim cleared his throat. "Actually, you know those two other guys that were sitting at the bar with you? Larry and Jake?"

She barely remembered their faces, but she recalled that they were both wearing highlighter-yellow shirts worn by road crew workers. "Yeah, I think so. What about them?" she asked.

"They are brothers. The last name is Henderson. I think they are renting the apartment just above the Cussler Bakery. You know where I'm talking about?" he asked.

She thought about the cupcake and pastry shop that pretty much made all the specialty cakes for every event in the town. It was about two blocks down from where she lived and a block off Main Street. "Yeah, I know the place. What about the brothers?"

"They have a six-hundred-and-fifty-dollar tab open at the bar. I told Heidi not to serve them anymore, but they got aggressive. It was a choice between her safety and beer—she decided to give them the beers and I don't blame her."

"What were you hoping I would do to help you?" Emily asked, wondering how wrapped up in trouble Tim wanted these guys to be.

"I was thinking you could bring them in on misdemeanor theft. Nothing major, just a slap on the wrist. If they pay their bill, don't bring them in and I won't press charges. Plus, you and I'll be square."

It annoyed her slightly that Tim thought he could so blatantly use her for his own gains, but she had found in the past that the people causing him problems were generally the same people causing her issues as well. Dollars to donuts, if she ran these Henderson brothers through her system, at least one of them probably had an open warrant.

"Just go ahead and send me the footage I need, and I'll take care of the brothers for you. Hopefully, the tab will be paid by the end of the day. If not, I'll let you know that they have been arrested and we will be waiting for word from you as to whether you want to press charges."

She could hear the clicking of computer keys in the background. "There you go. I just sent that e-mail off. I appreciate your help. Talk to you later."

Emily opened up her e-mail as soon as Tim hung up the phone. She was met with an image of the guy in the green-flannel shirt with his long ponytail and an unkempt beard. As before, she didn't recognize the man, and he didn't look like anyone she knew from within the town.

She zoomed in on the man's face and made sure it was not blurry before inserting it into her computer system and doing an image search. A variety of similar-looking men in mug shots popped up on her screen, but none of them looked identical to the man in the image from the bar.

She blew out a huff.

"Everything okay?" Cameron asked.

"Yeah. We are going to have to run an errand really quick though. That okay?"

Cameron nodded. "I'm not in a big rush to camp out." He chuckled.

She had tried to warn him about the reality of some situations, but there was nothing like being faced with someone who didn't want to help themselves. "Sex workers don't stay in that lifestyle forever—especially the ones who are doing it willingly. Most do get out of it, safely. There's not a lot of studies on it. Few want to talk about their pasts, but I would say that at least ninety percent of the women that go into that kind of lifestyle do come out alive. Thankfully, for those who are trafficked or are traumatized by what they experienced, there are a lot of nonprofit organizations out there trying to help."

He nodded, but she could tell that he was really bothered by what he had seen. She was, too, but over time she had become numbed to the problem and the shadow epidemic of human trafficking in the country.

That wasn't to say that it always hadn't been a problem, but it definitely increased thanks to the internet and cell phones.

"What's the errand we need to do?" he asked, pulling her from her melee of thoughts.

"Tim hooked me up with the image we needed for our BOLO, so I made the update." She clicked a few buttons on her computer and sent the image out statewide. She turned the computer so he could see what she had done. "Hopefully, this will help us to identify the guy we're looking for, and maybe another agency will pick him up. These actually tend to work pretty well. While we wait for the results on that, though, I told Tim we'd go pick up a couple of guys who ran out on their bar bill."

"That's what I thought I heard you say. I just thought

I got it wrong. It seems under your pay grade or something." He chuckled.

"Not everything we do is glitzy. A lot of the time, we are just gophers or therapists. Though, in your case we are actually doing something. You wouldn't believe some of the calls we get though. I'm not even kidding. One time we had a mom call about her son because he wouldn't eat his dinner."

He looked at her like she had lost her mind. "That is ridiculous."

She nodded. "It was definitely ridiculous, and the woman got off with a warning from Dispatch and we didn't respond, but that kind of thing happens. We show up to a lot of places where it's just two adults yelling at each other over something stupid. Usually something involving money or cars. Things that seem really big in the moment, but once people are calm, it's not so important." She turned on her blinker and it clicked as she turned left and they made their way toward the bakery.

The bakery was closed for the day and they climbed up the rickety white open stairs on the side of the building to the second-floor apartment's front door. Emily knocked on the door beside the four-panel glass windows covered with a curtain yellowed with age but she was sure had once been white maybe thirty years ago.

There was a grumble from inside the apartment, but she couldn't quite make out what the person inside had been saying.

"Flathead County Sheriff's Office! Open the door!" she ordered, using a tone that clearly meant business but was one decibel from yelling. If the guys didn't want to play ball, that would be what would come next.

A man came to the door. He was wearing the same

highlighter-yellow shirt that he had been wearing at The Mint and his face was still dirty. As the door swung open, she could see that he was holding a gold Coors Banquet beer can in his hand. "Something I can help you with?" he asked, looking surprised to see a sheriff's deputy standing on the other side of the door.

"Jake?" she asked.

"Larry." He lifted the can in his hand slightly. "Jake's in the shower. What did he do? He leave something at the bar?"

"No, actually I was hoping to ask you a few questions. You have a minute?"

The man gave her an appraising look, like he was trying to do a quick run-through of his life and think of every misdeed and decide if there was anything in his list of questionable actions that would get him arrested.

"As long as you work with me, you shouldn't have too much to worry about. I'd rather not drag you and your brother to jail tonight."

Larry gave her a little nod. "What do you need to know?" He stepped out of the door and onto the tiny porch with them. It was cramped with all three of them, but he closed the door behind him.

It made her wonder what he was hiding inside of his apartment, but without a search warrant or probable cause, there wasn't much she could do. "Do you recall the man from the bar, when we ran into you? He was seated a couple barstools down from you. Left in a hurry."

Larry nodded. "He was there when we got there after work. Didn't say much. Really nursed his beer. In fact, I think he only drank maybe one or two the whole time we were there."

"How long were you guys there?" she asked.

"Probably an hour and a half."

"Did he say anything to you?" She was half tempted to cross her fingers.

Larry leaned against the railing and crossed his arms over his chest in thought. "He said he was pissed off about something. Sounded like he was having problems with his girlfriend maybe."

"How do you know?"

"Some woman called him while we were sitting there. She sounded really upset. He was trying to calm her down. I don't really know what they were talking about, but he said he was gonna meet up with her later." He shrugged.

She tried to hide her excitement, but she shot Cameron a quick glance. He smiled at her like he, too, understood the significance of what the man had just told them. Perhaps the woman the man had been talking to was the same one who had left the hair tie in the barn. Maybe those two were responsible for killing Leonard and Ben. If she could get her hands on these two suspects, maybe she could get the answers Cameron so desperately needed and they could put this mystery to rest, and perhaps they could actually see if they could have a relationship.

There was a lot that rested on her ability to find answers.

"Did you catch either of their names?" she asked.

"I think he called her an odd woman's name. Something I hadn't heard before, but I couldn't tell you what it was. It was just really unique. I'd know it if I heard it again. though, you know?" Larry's face pinched slightly, like he felt bad that he couldn't be more help.

"No, that's good. Super helpful. Thank you for that," Emily said. "If you see the guy again, or if you remember the woman's name, I'd appreciate you giving me a call."

She reached into her chest pocket and pulled out one of her business cards and handed it to the man. "My name and my office number and extension are right there if you need to get in touch."

He took it and shoved it in his back pocket.

She turned to go and then remembered why they had come in the first place. "Oh, wait," she said, stopping. "I need you to run down to The Mint and pay your tab. If you don't, I'm going to come back here and arrest you and your brother. You got it?"

Larry's face paled. "Yes, ma'am… I mean, Officer."

"It's Deputy Monahan." She sent him a half smile, attempting to take some of the chill off her words. "And keep ahead of your bar tab. He's trying to make a living. He doesn't need to be chasing down bills all the time. Got it?"

Larry nodded. "Yes, Deputy Monahan."

"I'll be checking, so get it done soon. Like, within the hour." She motioned for Cameron to start heading down the stairs. "You guys have a good night. And don't forget to not drink and drive, you might want to get to walking so you can make it there on time."

She made her way downstairs as she heard the door to the apartment close behind her. All things considered, that unexpected stop had gone surprisingly well. As Cameron walked in front of her, she also got the added benefit of seeing his trademark Copenhagen can mark in the back pocket of his Wranglers. Not that she was just looking at that circular mark.

He really was a sexy man.

It would be incredible to be able to wake up with him every day.

Even though they had discussed boundaries before they had even gotten to the hotel, she couldn't help herself now that she was walking with him. She couldn't stand the thought of him not having a safe place to go for the night. She waited until they were both safely tucked inside her car before she said anything. "So, what do you think about spending another night at my house?"

"Are you worried that Larry's going to come for you in the night?" he teased. "I have to say I don't think he was really that upset. If anything, the most upset I think he was about anything was that he was going to have to pay his tab."

She laughed. "I'm just confused how anybody could get that big of a bar tab? That's impressive when all he drinks is beer. And not even expensive beer."

"I don't think it's about the type of beer, I think it's about the quantity and the number of times he hit that bar." He made a pinched expression. "I know that when I was going through my divorce there were a couple of weeks that I put up some impressive tab numbers, too. Thankfully, I can safely say those days are behind me."

She didn't want to ask if they truly were, or if the reality of his new life hadn't set in. She had a feeling that when grief struck, he would have a harder time of it than he anticipated. However, if she was lucky and she was allowed to follow her heart, perhaps she could be the one to stand by his side and support him through this turmoil.

Chapter Fourteen

It had been a long day and though it was only dinnertime, Cameron was ready to get out of the police cruiser. Those seats were not made to sit in all day, at least not the passenger side. He hadn't wanted to complain to Emily, who had seemed content driving around and doing what had to be done for her job, but he was relieved when she asked if he wanted to call it a day and go pick up Stacy.

They pulled up in front of the garage and she turned off the engine. "Usually, I like to leave my car outside or down the street. It tends to keep any problems to a minimum."

He could understand the thinking, but he was also a touch surprised that it didn't elicit more vandalism by teenagers who didn't understand the ramifications of their behaviors and were on a mission to impress their friends through acts of rebellion. He and Ben hadn't done anything quite so dumb when they had been teens, but they had come darned close.

Emily stepped out and closed the door and he followed. "Speaking of neighbors, here comes Penny," Emily said, and he looked in the direction she was indicating.

There, walking toward them, was an older woman who was wearing a T-shirt with Whiskey Helps emblazoned across the front and a flag on the sleeve. Her gray hair was cut short into a pixie, and she was wearing a pair of men's Levi's. Surprisingly, the matronly woman didn't have the little girl in tow.

"Is Stacy taking a nap?" Emily asked, glancing instinctively down at her watch and scowling.

"No," Penny grumbled. "Didn't you get my text message?"

"No," Emily said, pulling out her phone. "What happened? Is Stacy okay?"

"Yeah, she is fine. But your jerk of an ex was just here. He took her. Said it was his night to keep her. I tried to stall him, but you know how well he and I get along." She made a *pfft* sound and rolled her eyes. "You didn't say anything about him picking her up, and I didn't want to let her go, but he was being a real tool."

"That, I can believe." Emily closed her eyes as she exhaled. She tilted her head back and rolled her neck like she was trying to stave off a headache. "Tonight isn't Todd's night and he knows it. I appreciate you trying to stall him. I'm sure he was in a hurry since he knew I was probably getting off work any minute."

Cameron was surprised. Todd hadn't seemed like the type of guy, at least from what Emily had told him and from what he had first seen, to want to fight for time with his kid—or to spontaneously want extra overnight stays. However, this wasn't the time to bring it up as it would probably only make Penny feel even worse about letting the girl slip out of her fingers.

Emily was texting on her phone. From where he stood, he could see she was texting Todd, though he couldn't see exactly what she was saying. However, from the speed of her fingers, she was furious, and Todd was getting a screenful.

Penny stood there awkwardly staring at Emily. Cameron stepped up and offered her his hand in introduction. "By the way, Penny, my name is Cameron Trapper. Emily is working with me on a case. I've heard good things about you."

"The double homicide out at the cattle ranch?" Penny asked. She squinted her eyes and gave him a good once-over before she settled on his face. Her features relaxed as his gaze met hers.

"Yes, that's it." He would have asked how she knew, but it was a small town and his last name had been large at one time.

"Todd seemed to know that you spent the night here. He started to ask me to give him a call if you stayed again, but he stopped when he remembered who he was talking to," Penny said, puffing up her wide chest. "That man knows I wouldn't turn my steering wheel to save him if he was standing out in traffic."

Emily jerked her head up from her phone. "He said *what now*?"

Penny nodded. "You heard me right. I'm sure your daughter won't know not to say anything. Your goose is cooked if you wanted to keep that a secret."

Emily groaned. "Todd is going to have a field day with this one. I can't believe he already knew. What, does he have cameras planted around the house or something? *Gah…*" She went back to frantically texting.

He hoped she hadn't meant what she said, and she didn't really think Todd was the type of guy who would spy on her like that—or, more accurately, *stalk* her.

As for her texting, he couldn't tell whether Todd was replying, but it didn't seem to matter with the diatribe that Emily was sending.

He put his hand on her lower back. "Thanks for letting us know about Stacy. None of what happened was your fault. We will get it all handled, Penny." It felt strange handling the situation with the neighbor in Emily's stead, given the fact that Penny had far more time with the little girl than he had, but in this case, he had to help Emily even if it meant his own discomfort.

Penny gave him an appreciative nod as if she understood what he was attempting to do and didn't take his dismissal as a slight. "If you need anything, even in the middle of the night, I'm around. Again, I'm sorry I let her go. I know you said it's not my fault, but I wish I coulda done more to help."

Emily looked up from her phone. "Seriously, not your fault. Todd is just…well, *Todd.*" She said his name with a look of distaste.

Clearly, the women had spent many hours talking about the man and had developed a strong bond. He was glad that Emily had such a great neighbor and friend in her corner.

Penny turned to leave and head back to the blue two-story house next door that was similar in style but maybe a few years older than Emily's. As she reached the gate to her yard, she turned back. "And hey, don't forget, I have a gun if you need an extra shooter." She winked, but he could tell from the tone of her voice that she was only kind of kidding.

It made him like her even more.

Emily relaxed under his hand as Penny waved goodbye and walked into her house.

"I can't believe Todd did this. He couldn't give two—"

"Has he done this type of thing before?"

"Taken Stacy without letting me know?" She shook her head. "Never."

That was concerning. "Have you brought guys home after your divorce?"

She looked down at her phone, clicked off the screen and shoved it in her back pocket. "Who I have over here, or don't have over here, is none of Todd's business."

"That's not what I asked."

She looked away from him and then started to walk toward the door. "I haven't. Plus, Todd and I were supposed to meet with the mediator this week. We were modifying the parenting plan. He has been fighting for more hours. I think he is just playing games."

"And yet he just dropped her off to you during your workday?"

She shrugged. "He may have done that because he knew I wouldn't be able to watch her. That I'd have to give her to Penny. He could show the mediator that I don't actually care about my child—or something. Sometimes the things he does…well, they don't even make sense to me. He can be really manipulative and twisted."

"It sounds like you made the right decision in getting a divorce."

She nodded, but she didn't look back at him until she was inside. She waited for him to follow her in before she closed the door behind him and slipped the chain lock in place. "I've never had a regret when it comes to that. My only regret is that I have to put Stacy through this. He is using her like a pawn—clearly."

"You think he is just trying to mess with you by using her? Or do you think he really is trying to get more time with Stacy?"

She walked into the kitchen, poured herself a glass of water and downed it in one long drink. "I don't know what he is thinking, really. He isn't making anything easy. I thought all of this was behind me when the divorce was finalized. I didn't really think we would have to be back in lawyer's offices so soon after things were done and the decree was finalized. However, I think that he likes to control me this way."

Cameron had gone through so many emotions in the last day, but none was as strong as the anger he was feeling right now. He couldn't change or affect what had happened at the ranch, but he could still make a difference when it came to Emily and her daughter. Maybe he could still help them.

If he saw Todd again, he would be hard-pressed not to teach the guy one heck of a lesson.

"Has he texted you back?"

She shook her head.

"Do you know where he is living, or where he would have taken her?"

She sighed. "I already texted his mom. That is where he has been living. She hasn't seen him today, but she said she would let me know if they showed up. She is a bit of a drive away and, if they just left here, they may go and get dinner and then head out that way. He is probably ignoring me on purpose. It may be a couple hours until we hear anything."

"I know you probably don't want to go down this road, but if in a situation like this—without you guys agreeing on his taking Stacy with you—couldn't that constitute kidnapping?"

"We share custody, and it would get into a *he-said, she-said* battle because we are currently trying to renegotiate the parenting plan. It wouldn't go well, and it would end up looking bad for both of us if we ended up in court over it. It's best if we just get along—or, in this case, I just let him have his way." She ran her hand over the back of her neck as she looked up at the ceiling for a moment.

He felt bad for her.

"I'm sorry, Emily."

"Why are you sorry?" She frowned at him as she sat her glass back down on the counter.

"I'm sorry that I might be part of the reason he is messing with you and putting you and your daughter in danger. I didn't mean to make trouble in your private life. If you need, I can just head out. I can get a taxi to a different, more *upscale* hotel." He smiled, but even to him the action felt tired.

"You didn't cause this. Plus, I think Stacy is safe. I don't think Todd would do anything to hurt Stacy. He says he loves her."

"Are you sure that he wouldn't hurt her?" he asked, not wanting to scare her but concerned after everything that she had told him.

From the look on her face, she was thinking about all the ways Todd could hurt her when it came to her daughter. As a law enforcement officer, she had to know only too well what humans were capable of.

She chewed on her lip. "I know we just got here, but would you be okay if we swung over by Todd's place?"

As badly as he wanted to stay put and have a night alone with Emily, he nodded. "I thought you might want to do that." He opened the door and stepped outside. "I hope you know I'm worried about Stacy, too."

Since Todd hadn't left Penny's that long before they had arrived, it was possible that if they hurried, they could catch up with him on the highway.

She walked outside and they jogged to the car. They drove in stony silence for a few minutes until Emily finally cleared her throat. "Todd's mom's name is Alice. She's very nice, but Todd's dad was a lot like him."

"Do you mean cruel?" He couldn't believe that they had started out with him being interrogated by her and now he was the one asking the tough questions.

"I think that he was raised by a narcissistic father and some of those characteristics were passed down." She pulled onto the highway. "Alice wasn't overly heartbroken when her husband died of a heart attack a few years ago. She didn't even end up having a memorial service for him."

He could understand the woman's feelings for a variety of reasons. His thoughts went back to his father and his brother, and it suddenly felt like he had taken a fist straight to the gut.

For a moment, he had found reprieve from his own life, but the hit had come out of nowhere.

He'd heard that happened with grief—that it was a blow that would just randomly land. Whomever had told him that in the past had been right. He was just lucky he was sitting down, in an uncomfortable seat or not.

Emily reached over and put her hand out palm up, expectantly. "Things will get easier. At least, that's what Alice told me."

He had no idea how she knew what he was thinking about and what he was feeling, but as he took her hand and gripped her fingers protectively, he was glad that she could read him so well. "I appreciate hearing that."

"If you don't want to have a service for your brother, and you just want to do kind of what Alice did… I'll be there by your side if you want. Or, if you want to have a party…like an Irish send-off or a party for you, whatever you need. I've got you."

He laughed and some of the ache in his chest receded. She really was one hell of a woman.

"I'm thinking Jameson whiskey at The Mint. I bet Tim will throw us a deal if Larry actually pays his tab." He smiled.

"Heidi thought you were pretty cute," she teased.

He quirked his brow. "Oh, yeah?"

"You want me to get her number for you?"

He leaned back, surprised that she would offer such a thing when her hand was in his. "Are you kidding me right now? Why would you say something like that?"

She giggled. "What? Are you saying that you aren't interested in Heidi?" She gave him an appraising glance.

"Oh," he said, realizing what she was getting at. "I'm not interested in Heidi… There is a woman I am interested in, and I'm looking forward to getting to know her a lot better if and when she gives me a chance."

Emily smiled. "I think you have a pretty good shot with an answer like that."

He kissed her fingers and as he did, he was reminded of how much he appreciated being around her. She could turn his sorrow around with simply a smile and as long as he'd been dating, he couldn't remember a woman who'd ever had that type of effect on him. It had to mean something.

Her face went serious for a moment and she looked as though she wanted to say something, but instead, she sucked in a breath and squeezed his hand.

"You know, you can tell me anything. You can trust me," he said. "I'd hope by now I've proven myself."

She looked at him. "I know." Her phone buzzed and she let go of his hand as she pulled it out of her pocket. As she did, he spotted the name Bullock.

"Hello?" she answered.

There was a grumble of a man's voice. Bullock spoke

for a long time as Emily drove down the highway. She nodded a few times as she gave "yes, sirs" and "no, sirs" as if the detective could see her through the phone.

She told him about Stacy being taken. Bullock's tone grew deeper, and though he couldn't hear the man's words, Cameron could tell her colleague was angry.

As Emily pulled down a dirt road, she said her farewells and hung up with the detective. She stared out the window for a long minute as she drove. He wanted to ask her what he'd had to say, but it wasn't his place.

She pulled to a stop in front of an old ranch-style house. There was a '90s era Buick parked in front. Its front end was rusted and the rear bumper was crushed where it must have been in an accident sometime in the past.

"Is this Alice's place?" he asked.

Emily nodded, but she didn't speak as she got out of the car.

She was so quiet and so *off* that a lump formed in his stomach. Before Bullock had called, they had been talking about a relationship. Now she wasn't even speaking to him. He was confused. What had the detective found that could have upset her so much? Was it something at the scene that she didn't want to tell him?

He wasn't sure if she wanted him to stay in the car or follow her to the front door, so he stayed in place. Given the situation with Todd, he didn't want to make things worse or give the man more fodder for manipulation. If anything, he should have waited at the end of the road or something so, if Todd was here, he wouldn't have seen him in the car.

Then again, they had nothing to hide. Todd could take his judgment and anger and shove it. Emily was a grown and divorced woman who was free to date any man she wanted. Well, she was free to date any man she wasn't investigating.

Maybe *that* was what was bothering her. Perhaps Bullock had reminded her about the implications of their relationship if this case went to court and they were put on the stand and forced to answer questions presented by a defense attorney.

He'd already compromised her enough with Todd and her daughter, but dammit if he didn't want to still take her in his arms and make everything bad that was happening in their lives disappear.

Chapter Fifteen

Emily stood on Alice's front porch for a long moment. She hesitated to knock on the door. She knew Alice had undoubtedly heard them drive up, may even have watched them through a crack in the window coverings.

Yet she wasn't ready to face her former mother-in-law.

It wasn't that she didn't like Alice—in fact, she was the only person in Todd's family she could still have a somewhat amiable conversation with. Rather, it was the fact that she had to be here at all that was rubbing her the wrong way. There were a ton of other things she could have been doing and yet Alice's son had insisted on creating problems where there shouldn't have been any.

Emily thought about the conversation she'd had with Cameron. She might have been wrong in telling him the truth about Todd and his manipulative behaviors. It was too much, too soon. She wasn't a girl who needed rescuing, or pity. At the same time, she didn't want Cameron thinking that she was a bad mom or that this was some strange game Todd was playing in an attempt to win her back.

She looked at the car one more time and Cameron smiled up at her. He was a good man. If she was in a better place in her life, he would have been the perfect guy. Her mind flashed to their kiss. That kiss had been the most perfect moment in her life, aside from moments with her daughter, in years.

She couldn't think about that now. She had to focus on the safety of her daughter. And she had to get things under control with Todd. Obviously, he wanted to create problems. Whether it was because of Cameron or because of something else that he had drummed up in his mind, it appeared as though he was making it his mission to punish her.

Todd's truck wasn't outside, but that didn't mean Stacy wasn't there. Knowing him, he'd grabbed her and then just handed her off to his mother after he'd put on a big show to make himself look better. For all she knew, maybe he had a new woman in his life and that was what this was all about. Or it could have been for the judge, or a combination of both. Who knew with Todd.

She knocked on the door, violently hoping that Stacy would come running to answer. She was met with the sound of heavy footfalls from the other side of the closed door. The locks clicked and as the door creaked open, Alice came into view. She was wearing a hot-pink body suit that clung to her like Saran wrap. For being in her late sixties, she looked great.

Alice looked surprised to see her. "Emily, what's happening?"

"I know you said you'd give us a call if Todd showed up, but I'm really worried about Stacy. Have you heard from or seen them at all?"

Alice put her hand on her hip as she stared out at Cameron. She furrowed her brow and, for a moment, she looked a lot like her son.

"Honey," she said, taking her by the arm and leading

her inside as she shut the door behind them—but not before throwing one more look of disgust out at Cameron.

Alice motioned for her to follow her into the kitchen. The house was modular, the kind that had been produced in the late '90s and sold in mass quantities. While it was nice, it had already started to show signs of breaking down faster than a traditionally built home. Alice had needed to replace the roof and some of the trusses, which, she'd explained to Emily, had cost her nearly as much as the house had originally cost to purchase.

In the corner of the living room, there was a plastic Playskool toy box overflowing with toys, most of which Emily recognized as hand-me-downs from when Todd had been a child and were now Stacy's. On top was a Hulk fist that was faded and stitched where Todd had once punched it through a bathroom mirror.

Looking back, she had made some horrible decisions in her life. It wasn't like there hadn't been plenty of red flags when it came to Todd, she had just been too blind and too young to see them.

Alice's kitchen was barely stocked, as per usual. But she had her trademark bottle of Tito's and club soda in the refrigerator, which she grabbed out and started to pour without asking. She handed a glass of vodka and soda to Emily before pouring herself one as well.

"I know you like lime in yours, but I'm fresh out. Sorry." She didn't sound like she really cared. If anything, she sounded like she was glad that Emily had provided her with an excuse to pour a drink.

If Todd was her son, she'd want to drink, too. She wondered if Alice was embarrassed about her son's behavior, and that was where her reaction was stemming from.

"Thanks for the drink," Emily said, raising the glass but

not taking a sip as she was still in uniform even though she was off the clock. "You didn't answer my question though. Have you heard from your son?"

Alice didn't seem to be able to meet her eyes. It didn't help quell the fear Emily was feeling. "If you know something, Alice, please tell me. You must understand how I'm feeling. My child is missing."

Alice pinched the bridge of her nose and let out a long sigh. She closed her eyes and leaned against the counter, letting it support her weight. "He called right before you got here. I talked to him about what was going on. He didn't want me to tell you, but he is running up to Canada."

Emily's hand holding the drink started to shake with rage and the liquid sloshed over her fingers, forcing her to put the glass down on the counter. Now it was Emily who was forced to put both hands on the surface to hold herself in place. She was going to kill him.

How could her ex-husband kidnap their child and abscond to Canada? What if he never came back? She'd heard horror stories about mothers and fathers being torn from children's lives forever just like this. Once a child left the country, it was incredibly difficult and very expensive to get them back. Todd knew it, too.

He had stolen her child.

"Where did he go?" she asked, trying not to let her fear and anger turn to tears.

"He wanted to take her fishing in Fernie," Alice said.

"Fishing? Seriously?" Emily couldn't think of more than a handful of times Todd had ever gone fishing. And he had certainly never taken Stacy fishing before. She didn't even have a rod. It made all her warning bells go off.

"Do you know where he's staying there?" Emily asked, trying to stay calm. She would need as much information as she could get to give to the Royal Canadian Mounted Police in order to get her daughter back.

Alice put her hand on top of Emily's. "I don't know if this is going to make you feel better or not, but Todd is seeing a new woman. She lives up in Fernie. I think that is why he's really going up there."

Emily let out a long exhale. Strangely enough, the fact that her ex-husband was dating someone new was actually a relief. It didn't feel quite so much like he was trying to steal her daughter. They weren't out of the woods; he still had to come back with her. But she was less afraid that they would be gone forever. Todd was still Todd.

"So, you don't think he's really fishing?" She looked over at Alice and finally decided to take a long drink from the proffered vodka. One drink wouldn't hurt.

"I think the only thing he's really fishing for is his new girlfriend's approval. Though he may or may not actually go fishing to impress her. You know how these things work." She gave half-hearted shrug and a wave of the hand.

If he was trying to impress a new woman, he wouldn't want Stacy to get hurt and she found comfort in the thought. At least that was one fear that she could take off her plate.

"Do you know when he was planning on coming back?" she asked. "When does he have to work?"

"I think he works in a couple days, but I'm just taking a guess." Alice looked over at the calendar hanging on the wall like it would hold the answer, but it showed nothing. "Here's the deal, honey. You and I both know that Todd loves your daughter—regardless of the mess you two have going. He screwed up here. He shouldn't have taken her without talking to you first, but he isn't great at dealing with things sometimes."

"He can't just take my daughter."

"She's his daughter, too."

Rage roiled within her. Alice wasn't wrong, and she wasn't going to argue with her over that point. However, there were rules about healthy parenting and co-parenting and until he learned to follow them, she would have to take the steps necessary to make sure he would never be able to pull something like this again.

If Emily could prove that Stacy had gone with him unwillingly, she could wrap him up with possible kidnapping charges. Then she could have an Amber Alert placed for Stacy. And then, hopefully, her daughter could be back in her arms by the end of the night. She would also probably never have to worry about sharing custody with Todd—and he would likely be heading for prison.

The other options she had were to have him charged with parental interference when he got back. Or, have nothing happen at all through the courts and legal system, and they could simply talk and go over what he could and couldn't do in the future.

She pulled out her phone and texted him again, begging him to respond and to let her know where he was with Stacy and when they would be back. Her response would be based on his—the ball was in his court.

With her anger what it was, she wanted to string him up. However, between the two of them, she had to be the responsible and levelheaded parent. And she had to keep in mind what was truly best for Stacy. She wasn't totally convinced that included time with her father at this present second, but maybe Emily would change when her daughter was safely tucked back in her arms.

Todd just didn't think sometimes, or ever, depending on who a person asked.

She sighed and put her phone back in her pocket.

Alice emptied her glass and poured herself another.

"Wait," Emily said, pushing her nearly full glass over. "You can have mine. I'm not going to finish it. I need to go. We just both need to hope that Todd makes the right choice and Stacy is returned safe."

Chapter Sixteen

Emily walked into her house, stripped off her utility belt and laid it down on the table next to the front door. It felt good to feel the weight leave her hips and lower back. She leaned forward, shifting her weight until she heard popping sounds.

It had been one hell of a long day.

"It will all be okay. I'm sure he'll be back tomorrow. He has to know that his ass is on the line. Did you tell him you are going to get law enforcement involved if he doesn't respond?" Cameron asked, walking in behind her and closing her front door.

She watched his tanned hands work as he slid the gold chain into place, securing the front door. It was silly to put so much faith in such a silly little chain to keep her safe. A chain wasn't about to stop someone who was hell-bent on coming into her house if they wanted. Yet it helped her sleep better at night. It was funny how a person told themselves trivial lies in order to comfort themselves, even when they knew better.

It was so much like what she was telling herself about Todd right now.

"Yes, he'll be back. He knows what he's doing is wrong." She smiled, wishing she had her own bottle of Tito's here to quell all her nerves. There would be no sleep in her world tonight. Stacy was safe, but it killed Emily that she didn't know where exactly she was.

Cameron took her by the hand. He walked her into the living room and stood her by the couch. He put his hands down on her hips. "I promise you, I'm not going to do anything you don't ask for or want. I am only going to try to be here for you. Okay?"

Every part of her sparked. Energy coursed through her body and she clenched with lust. Yet she held back. She didn't need more chaos, but she could let him supplicate her tonight and help her relax.

He reached toward her. "Is it okay if I unbutton your shirt?" he asked, smiling.

She sucked her bottom lip into her mouth and she stepped back until she touched the top of the couch, where she rested her weight. She nodded.

He started at the top button. He slowly moved the smooth little plastic piece through the threaded hole with his thick, callused fingers before moving to the next and the next. She watched his hands work. There was something so sexy about his hands. They were dark and tanned; the color of treated leather.

His fingernails were thick and kept short, but round and clean. The tips of his fingers were rough from years of hard work and they made a scraping sound as he worked against the polyester fabric of her shirt. The soft sound made her body contract and ache as she thought of those textured fingers working her in more forbidden places.

She made a soft, moaning groan as she reached up and threaded her fingers through his hair and lifted his cowboy hat. With her left hand, she pulled it off and flung it over to the recliner. He could get that later.

He pulled her shirt loose from her pants forcibly, tugging and making her panties pull against her. She giggled at the sweet and welcome sensation.

"I should have guessed that you liked it just a touch hard." He smirked, the look on his face so sexy that she wanted to rip his clothes off and finish him, but she stopped herself.

He was only there to help her relax. That didn't mean they were taking things to the bedroom—unless she decided.

She was in control.

Cameron reached up and slid the shirt free of her shoulders and down off her arms. It tickled her skin, making her flesh prickle as he pulled it free. He folded it delicately as he sat it on the top of the couch beside her, taking his time, as if he was enjoying making her wait.

He smiled at her. "May I remove your gun?" he asked, pointing at her Glock in the bellyband at her waist.

She nodded.

He waggled his finger, motioning for her to turn slightly so he could reach behind her to loosen the Velcro. It made a ripping sound as he pulled it loose and removed the thick elastic band. He lifted the gun free of her and the cool evening air flowed against her sweaty skin. It always felt so strange taking that gun off. She felt at her most vulnerable—even being without clothing was less uncomfortable than being without a weapon.

She wanted to reach for it for a brief second, and her fingers instinctively moved. However, she stopped herself as she watched him carefully wrap the gun in the bellyband and place it gently on top of her shirt, the barrel facing away from them.

Reaching up, she ran her hand over her skin feeling

the sweaty spot where the gun had sat. It was strange how something so foreign could become part of a person. It was like a limb and, even though it was not there, she could still feel its phantom weight.

He knelt in front of her and untied her boots. She put her hands on his shoulders to steady herself and she could feel his well-defined muscles working. The sensation did nothing for her resolve to keep him from her bed.

Pulling her boots free, he walked them over to the front door and, bending over, he sat them straight and aligned on the mat. She stared at his round ass, the mark on his jeans more noticeable than ever. The funny thing was, she had never seen him chew. Did they make jeans with the mark on them now?

He readjusted the boots, making the toes touch. It seemed a little overdone, and it made her wonder if he knew she was watching him and he was showing off for her. It made her like him more. It wasn't as though he needed to try for that to happen; she liked him so much already it was becoming painful.

He stood up and turned to face her, sending her his trademark smirk. "What happens next is completely up to you. I can rub your feet, or I can rub your back. That is, if you'd like me to."

He knew damn well she wasn't going to pass an offer like that up. If he was like most guys, this massage would last about two minutes and then it would turn into something else entirely. However, feeling the way she was, it may not have been Cameron leading things in that direction. In fact, he was the one who wasn't pushing things that way.

She wasn't used to having this kind of control over men. She could get used to it.

"Let's take a shower. Then my room," she said, pointing down the hall.

"Whoa." He actually looked surprised at her being so forward. "Are you sure that's where you wanna go?"

"I didn't say let's get naked. I just wanna relax and feel the water on my skin. If you're going to rub my back, it seems like the best place." She sent him a coy smile that she hoped was at least half as sexy as the one he was giving her.

Two could play his teasing game.

She took him by the hand, lacing their fingers together and walked in front of him. She turned around and walked backward down the hall, playfully smiling at him as she pulled her hair free of her ponytail and brushed it loose with her fingers so it fell freely over her shoulders.

It felt good to have it brush against her skin.

He stared at her as she moved her hips and they neared the bathroom. "Do you have any freaking clue how beautiful you are? Has anyone ever told you?"

She shook her head.

"You are," he said, sounding a little breathless. "You are the most beautiful woman I have ever seen. You are stunning."

She tried not to blush, but the way he was looking at her together with his words made the heat rise in her cheeks. There was no doubt he meant what he was saying, and it made her swoon.

This man was perfect. He was everything she wanted.

Well, except maybe one thing.

Truth be told, as much as she appreciated a man who respected her boundaries and didn't want to take things any further than she felt comfortable, she also wanted a man who knew what he wanted and wasn't afraid to take it—and that also meant *her*.

Confused by all her feelings, wants and desires, she turned away from him and walked into her bathroom and turned on the shower. It was just as she had left it this morning, her makeup lined up according to usage and everything in its exact place.

She pulled out an extra fluffy white towel and laid it on the counter for him.

If she was about to take the next step with Cameron, she wanted to make sure she was giving it the right amount of thought and making a good decision.

Then again, who was she kidding? She had made the decision that she would to take things to the next level with him the minute she'd let him start undressing her. However, she wasn't going to be the one to make the first move. If he didn't take what he wanted, she wasn't going to ask. She wasn't the type of woman who wanted to be dominant, at least not usually.

She turned her back to him as she looked in the mirror and pushed a wayward hair behind her ear. He started to massage her back over her sweaty tank top, but the ridges of her shirt pressed into her skin.

She wanted to take it off, but the idea went against her resolve.

He kept rubbing, moving down to her hips, then down her to her lower back. His touch felt so good, and she felt her body relaxing against the counter in front of her. This was what she needed.

She became so relaxed she closed her eyes, she wasn't sure how she was still standing, but she didn't care.

He moved up to her back, starting on her shoulders again. "If you're comfortable, you can take off some of

your extra clothes. I could do a better job in the shower—
with a little lather." He sent her a sexy smile in the mirror.

"So, you want to see me naked?" She was done playing.

In or out?

He chuckled. "I don't just want to see you naked. I want
to be buried between your thighs."

Game on.

She moved away from his touch and turned around to
face him. In one fluid motion, she pulled her tank top over
her head, exposing her black bra. Reaching down to her
pants, she unbuttoned the top.

"Stop right there," he ordered.

She looked up with wide eyes. Had he changed his mind
when he'd seen her take off her top?

He folded her into his arms, taking his lips with hers
and devouring her. She forgot everything but his touch
and the way his warm body felt against her exposed skin.

His tongue flicked against hers, making her mind race
to all the places his tongue could travel on her body...and
all the things he could make her feel.

She wanted it all—all of him.

"I undress you, if you are giving me the honor of you."

His words were so proper and so perfect, and she loved
his perspective. She had lost the reality that giving her
body to another person was just that—an honor. In return,
his giving his to her was the same. Their choosing to do
this would mean something; it wouldn't be like most re-
lationships of this generation—it wouldn't be a one-night
stand, it wouldn't be meaningless sex or a situationship.

She leaned in and their kiss met in the middle.

She unbuttoned his shirt and pushed it off his shoulders
and let it hit the floor behind him, then she unzipped his
pants. She pushed them down, exposing his blue boxers,

which were working hard to hold his body in check. He was blessed with more than any man she had ever seen, so much that it made her heart race. Hopefully, their bodies would fit in the ways they both needed.

He looked to her for approval.

"Yes," she said, smiling wide. "Oh...*yes*."

He beamed. "I'm glad you like what you see."

She couldn't wait to feel him.

He reached for her and unbound her pants and let them fall atop his. Her panties were almost the same color as his boxers, and it seemed like a good sign. He pulled off his boxers.

Cameron ran his finger along the top of her panties and pulled her closer, making her gasp. He kissed her as he pushed his fingers down until he found her. He ran his fingers over her, rubbing her and making her moan in his mouth.

He pulled his hand out of her panties. He moved and pulled her panties down her legs.

They stepped inside the shower and let the warm water wash over their bodies as they found each other.

He worked her like she was a joystick, rolling and rubbing in just the right ways. She pressed into his hand, making him move harder against her and his hand filled with water and intensified the sensation. "More," she begged.

Her head swam with endorphins. He smiled at her as pressed her body against the wall and he dropped to his knees in front of her and then put her left leg over his shoulder.

His mouth found her.

She pressed her head back against the wall, floating on the sensation of his tasting her. Just when she thought it couldn't get better, he stood up and found her with his body. He pressed inside her, making her gasp.

He moved slowly at first, letting her get used to him. She moved together with him, wrapping her legs around him, pulling him deeper and reveling in the sweet pain that came with him filling every space within her.

He felt so good, and he grew harder inside her, making her wonder if he was close. Just as she wondered if he was going to finish, he paused and—without pulling out—he moved to the floor of the shower until she was atop and the water was pouring down her back.

She was riding her cowboy like he was her bronc, and she loved every single second of it. But as she rolled her hips, she knew she wouldn't last long. He fit her perfectly, as if he was made just for her.

Every cell of her body begged for release as the pressure intensified. She started to slow, but instead of letting her wait, Cameron took hold of her hips and moved her body for her, driving her with him. With his hands strong on her hips, he worked her body until they finished, their bodies shaking together.

Chapter Seventeen

Last night was hands down the best of his life—and not just because of the sex, but that had been the best, too. Cameron was busy doing their breakfast dishes as Emily came down the hallway still drying her hair with a towel after this morning's shower—which had only reminded her of all the positions he'd had her in only hours before.

"Thanks for doing that. You didn't need to clean up." She walked over and kissed him on the cheek like this was just their normal morning.

They were the picture of domestic bliss and he loved it. This was definitely something he could get used to.

"Did you talk to Bullock?" he asked.

She wrapped the towel around her head. Even without a single drop of makeup and without her hair done, she was just as beautiful as the first moment he had seen her. She would always be.

"Yeah, I talked to him for a few before your shower. They found the guy from the bar, his name is Eli Schuster."

"Did they arrest him?"

"Yes, but not for the murders. They found him at the Arrow Lodge. He was one of the *guests*. The woman at the bar was the one we had seen before at the hotel." She sighed. "They are going to question him about everything, but as of now, it doesn't sound like he knows anything."

"What happened to the woman?"

She shrugged. "On another note, Bullock has decided to open your ranch back up so you can get back in for your animals." There was a touch of sadness in her voice.

He understood; the sadness was echoed in his soul. He nodded as if it was all he could do.

"He also said more of the fingerprints came back. It was actually kind of weird." She grabbed a rag and started to wipe down the countertop.

"What do you mean *weird*?"

She shrugged. "Well, it's not a huge surprise, but a lot of the fingerprints came back both as yours and as Trevor's."

He nodded. "Yeah. I'm in the house quite a bit. Though, I hadn't been in there that morning."

"I recalled you saying that." She wiped down the stove and walked over to rinse the rag before hanging it over the faucet. "When was the last time you know Trevor was in the house?"

He shrugged. "Trevor had his kid that day. He may have gone in there that morning, but I don't know. Did Bullock question him? If he hasn't, I'm sure I can get Trevor to come in and talk to him."

"Yeah, let's set that up. I am sure once we do, we can make sense of why he had so many prints in the house."

"So, none of that is really weird…" he continued, pressing her.

"Well, there is another set of prints that aren't coming up as linked to anyone in our database. They searched all night."

"That's good, isn't it?" he asked, pushing the dishwasher

closed and wiping off his hands. The news brought him a renewed sense of excitement.

"It is, but it isn't. We know that it is very possible there is someone else that may be involved with their deaths, and you may be cleared. However, it means that we have nowhere to start in identifying them. To get them, we will just have to get lucky."

"Is there a way you can figure out if a fingerprint is a man or a woman's, you know…based on size or something?" He felt stupid for asking, but he honestly didn't know.

"No, because sizes vary by person—even age. There are a tremendous number of variables."

He nodded. It made complete sense.

"But, on another positive note, if we bring someone in and they match, we are in the money." She smiled widely and it brought thoughts of her on top of him flash in his mind.

She was a beautiful woman.

"If I've learned anything in the last twelve hours, it's that I'm a very lucky man." He walked behind her and put his hand on her hip, kissing her neck.

She put her hand on the side of his face and leaned into his kiss as she smiled. "I'm the lucky one." She kissed him. "I do need to get to work though. Plus, I need to try to get in touch with Todd again. He hasn't texted, but he's been posting pictures of Stacy on social media."

It was something. At least they could find some comfort in the fact that her daughter was safe, even though her ex was a total jerk. He was impressed with how levelheaded she was in handling the situation. He didn't know how he would have been, as he didn't have a child himself and he certainly wasn't in a position that he could pass judgment.

However, he was furious for Emily and Stacy wasn't even his daughter.

He considered that for a moment.

What would it be like to have a child? And what about a child that wasn't biologically his?

He wouldn't care who the baby belonged to by genes. He would love them the same—especially Stacy. He already loved her. And as for her mom...

He looked over at Emily and smiled.

She smiled at him. "I'm going to go finish my hair, then we can hit the road. You ready?"

He nodded, but the truth was that he never wanted to leave this stolen moment of bliss. He didn't want to go back to the ranch. If it wasn't for his family's honor, their legacy and the need to find justice, he would have been happy to live here, waiting for Stacy to be returned, forever.

He watched her as she made her way to the bedroom.

While he waited, he called Trevor.

He answered on the second ring even though it was early in the morning. "How's it going, man?"

"Good. You running the cattle up today?" he asked.

"I was planning on it. Did you want to join me?"

Cameron stared down the hallway. He had never missed a chance to move the cattle. It was one of the most fun experiences of the year. It was a lot of work and Trevor would need the extra hands, but he also didn't want to leave Emily—especially when she still hadn't heard from Todd about her daughter.

"I'll let you know."

"Where are you?" Trevor asked.

He looked at Stacy's newborn announcement that was framed and hanging in the hallway. "I'm working on the murders."

"So, you're with *her*." Trevor chuckled. "It's okay. She's hot. I get it."

"Whatever, man. You just worry about the cows. They need to get up to the mountains."

"They aren't the only ones thinking about mountains right now," Trevor said, laughing. "Enjoy those peaks. You know where to find me." He hung up the phone.

It didn't take long for Emily to get ready and when she came out, her hair was pulled tight against her head. She walked to the front door and put on her boots, then came over to the couch and picked up her bellyband and strapped it around her waist and followed it with her utility belt and her uniform shirt.

"Who were you talking to?" she asked.

"Trevor." He smiled. "He is going to move the cows for me."

She nodded. "I bet you're relieved. I know you've been worried about them."

"Every day we wait is a day that we may end up having to possibly hay them in the winter. It's lost revenues. My dad already cost us a ton of money—or at least I thought he had." His thoughts went to the strange money exchanges in his father's bank account. So many things just didn't make sense. "Did Bullock look into my father's financial records?"

"I bet. I haven't asked him, but that is always one of the first things they pull. That, and cell phone records. Don't worry, he is pretty thorough. He's good at his job."

"I have no doubt. He seems like he is patient with you, like he is trying to bring you up the ranks."

"He is a good teacher. I don't know about wanting to bring me up, but I do think he wants to make sure I'm good at my job and an asset to the team. My being proficient is good for everyone and good for families."

"Would you want to be a detective?" he asked.

She thought for a moment. "It would be a lot of extra work and responsibility, and I'm not sure how it would affect my time with Stacy, but if I could do it without interfering with my parenting, yes. I enjoy the work."

"You are great at it," he said.

Smiling at him, she clicked her belt and adjusted everything into place. "And you are a fantastic man."

As they made their way outside, Emily's phone rang. She stopped midstride. "Todd! Where the hell are you?" she exclaimed, answering the phone.

As badly as Cameron wanted to listen in on the phone call, it wasn't his business. He kept walking and leaned against her cruiser, waiting for her. From the expression on her face as she spoke to her ex-husband, she was furious. She had every right.

He wanted to reach through the phone for her.

At least the man was calling. For once, he was doing something right.

Emily looked over at him and put her finger up, indicating that she would just be a second. He waved her off. She could take just as much time as she needed. That man needed a tongue-lashing that only she could adequately provide.

He kept catching expletives, and it made him smile. The man deserved to be called every name in the book. After a few minutes, some of her anger seemed to abate and from what he could hear, it sounded as though Todd was on his way back over the border. Fernie was only a three-hour drive from where they were, so it wouldn't take long for Stacy to be back home and safe.

He still couldn't believe that the man had taken the little girl over an international border without clear permission from her mother. Until now, he hadn't even thought to ask her about a passport, but Todd must have had one for Stacy. In the end, it didn't matter. All that mattered was he had done what he had done. Now Stacy just needed to remain safe. Until she was back, though, he couldn't relax. Clearly, Todd wasn't the type of person Cam could assume would make the right decisions.

He couldn't take anything for granted with this guy, and neither could Emily.

She hung up the phone. Before putting it away, she made a quick call to Penny. He tried not to listen in, but he could hear her letting her neighbor know to keep an eye out for Todd in case he decided to swing by her house and drop Stacy off without warning. Penny said something and she sounded relieved in the background as they said goodbye.

Emily shoved the phone back into her back pocket. She lifted her chin up toward the sky, closing her eyes. She let out a long breath and it sounded almost like a growl. She needed a moment, and he respected that.

After she collected herself, she made her way over to him and they both got into the car in relative silence. "Well, at least Alice was right. Todd was just trying to impress some chick. I'm sure I'm not done having it out with him. But he should have Stacy home soon."

"I'm glad to hear it."

"He also knew that you would spend the night, again. Apparently, he has his spies working overtime." She put the car into gear and got the show on the road.

He didn't know what to say about their being watched. However, it made him deeply uncomfortable. It was a small town, and it wasn't like his truck was outside. So, whomever was feeding Todd information had to have seen him walk into her house or else they had been looking in a window. Either way, people were paying close attention.

"I'm sorry, Emily. I shouldn't have stayed here last night, but I'm not sorry about what happened between us. I won't apologize for that. Ever." He reached his hand over and she slipped hers in his.

"And you don't have to. That was incredible. I didn't know I could feel like that. You awaken parts of me..." The car accelerated slightly. "As for spies, I don't care. He's going to do whatever he's going to do anyways. I still have the upper hand. And it's not like he's not dating someone, too."

Cameron grinned. He loved that she said they were dating. He wasn't sure that he wanted to call it to her attention though. "Exactly. Screw him."

She tapped her fingers on the steering wheel.

When they arrived at the ranch, theirs was the only police vehicle. Though he had known that it had been cleared, and it was no longer considered a crime scene, it still felt like one. He half expected Detective Bullock to come walking out of the barn as they stopped.

Trevor's pickup was parked beside the barn, where he must have been inside getting ready to take the cattle out.

"I was hoping to do a walk-through in the house, do you mind?" Emily asked. "I've gone through the pictures a ton of times, but I feel like I'm missing something."

He nodded. "Help yourself. In fact, I'll go in with you. I haven't been in the house since before everything happened. I've been wondering what everything looks like and what I was going to have to deal with when I got back inside."

"I should warn you," she said, "we don't clean up crime

scenes. So, your house is probably going to be a mess. I know there was some blood where your brother went down. You need to be prepared for what you might walk into." She put her hand on his and gave it a squeeze before letting it fall away.

"I just appreciate you being here. This would be a hell of a thing having to face it alone."

She nodded and, as she moved, a tendril of hair fell into her face, the effect making her look less like a deputy and more like the woman he had come to know so well last night.

"Before we run in there, though, let's check on Trevor." He pointed at the barn. "Maybe, if you're not too busy, we can help him move the cattle. It's a lot easier with more hands, but I know you have to work and there's a lot of things you need to do. So don't feel pressured. I'd much rather you find the people that killed my family." His words came out in a hurry.

She sent him a gentle, understanding smile, like she understood the mix of feelings he was experiencing. "Sure, and if you want, we can also go into the house when we get back. If you're not ready to deal with this and see what's waiting… I understand. It's a lot."

Until she had said that, he hadn't realized that his wanting to go see Trevor was his way of avoiding the inevitable. Yet she was right. He wasn't sure he was ready to walk into that living room—he could still envision his brother's lifeless eyes staring at him. They would haunt him for years.

He could only imagine what was going to happen to him when he got in the house that now had sat with the scent of death for a few days and the blood smear near the doorway leading to the bedrooms. He had no idea how he would react when he had to wipe the bloody handprints off the walls.

The thought made his stomach churn.

As they made their way into the barn, Trevor was nowhere in sight. None of the horses or tack was missing. Cam glanced out into the parking area and noticed, for the first time, that one of the big ranch trucks with the horse trailer was gone.

It made sense; Trevor may have had to grab another hand from a neighboring ranch to help him on the drive since he thought he may have been working alone. Cameron would have done the same thing.

It was only a couple of miles' ride to where they had to move the cattle, but Trevor had probably taken the trailer and dropped it up there to help transport them back after the drive and was having the other hand give him a ride back to where they'd get the horses together.

He shrugged it off. Trevor knew exactly what he was doing. Cam trusted him implicitly.

And yet his thoughts went back to the bloody handprint.

"Didn't you say that some of the fingerprints on the scene came back as Trevor's?" he asked.

Emily walked up beside him. "Yes, why?"

"Where were his fingerprints found?" he asked.

She took out her phone and pulled up some information. "According to Bullock, it was around the living room, door handles… Normal locations one would expect for a guy that was coming and going from the house. It was mostly in the same areas where we found yours."

"Hmm." That was good; it made him feel more at ease. "Did they get any prints from the bloody handprint on the wall? Can you all do that from blood?"

She nodded. "Of course. Yeah, we got some. One set of bloody handprints was your brother's. Another handprint we located was belonging to that unknown source."

"But it wasn't Trevor's?" he asked directly.

She frowned, looking concerned. "You haven't mentioned that he would have been capable of this before. Are you seriously concerned that he may have done this? Or that he may have played a role in their deaths?"

He ran his hands over his face in exasperation. "I don't know what to think. My mind's all over the place."

She looked at him for a long moment, assessing him. "Yeah, let's just go for a ride today. The house can wait. Bullock has everything in motion for your case. And Stacy's on her way home. We have cell phone service the whole ride, right?"

"I think so, but I don't always use my phone while we're doing these kinds of things."

"I'm only worried that if someone reaches out about that BOLO, I need to be able to be in contact with the outside world."

Cell service was a legitimate concern in the mountains of Montana. "If we are out of service, we won't be for very long. Is that okay? If not, we can just work on cleaning up the house." Even as he said the words, his entire body tightened with anxiety.

She shook her head. "Babe, last night you rescued me from my fear and anger. Today it's my turn to rescue you."

Chapter Eighteen

Emily hadn't ridden a horse in years, and she shifted in the saddle in an attempt to keep it from rubbing uncomfortably against her tailbone. If they were going to go too far, she would have to change some things or she would have one heck of a saddle sore. The leather creaked as she moved and the horse flicked its ears back at her, not liking her movement.

She was riding Cameron's horse, Ginger, who was ironically a bay mare. She was a sweetheart. When Emily had come up to her, the bay had remembered her and gently nuzzled her face. She'd never considered herself a horse person, but this horse was one that could get her to change her mind. She ran her hand down the mare's neck and gave her a soft pat.

The horse blew out a relaxed breath as she walked forward, her gait smooth and even.

She was a dream to ride, or at least she would be if it weren't for the ill-fitting saddle.

If she was ever really going to consider getting more involved with Cameron, and if it became something more permanent—she blushed at the thought—she would need to start her transition to rancher's girlfriend with the purchase of a new saddle.

Cameron looked over his shoulder at her. "You're doing okay back there?"

"Just trying to find my sea legs." She smiled.

He slowed his mare down so their horses were side by side. "You just want to make sure that you engage your core. You want to focus on sitting up straight and keeping the weight off your back pockets. The only part that should be moving on you is your hip joints and it should be moving with the horse. Put your heels down, knee out in the stirrup. And we lead with our pelvis and thighs more than we do with the bit. Horses have really sensitive mouths, so you don't have to move the reins much to make them listen."

At least now she understood why the horse was having such a problem with her shifting haphazardly in the saddle. It made her feel worse about her discomfort. Without being free to shift when necessary to alleviate rubbing, she wasn't sure what she was going to do. It looked like it was about to be a very long day.

Emily focused on her posture and engaged her core. As she did, she found she wiggled less in the saddle and she sat up straighter. There was less rubbing.

Had he noticed that she was rubbing? Or had he just known she was going to have problems?

Regardless, she appreciated he was there to help before things took a turn for the worse and she wasn't able to walk when she got down.

With his simple suggestions, the pain Emily had been experiencing abated. It wasn't gone completely, but it was a lot better. Even her knees were feeling better. She definitely had a lot to learn.

They made their way deep into the pasture and through a series of gates, closing all of them behind themselves.

When they reached the last pasture, they came upon a large herd of Black Angus cattle. At least, she assumed they were Black Angus; they were large and black and, as far as she knew, that was what they were called.

"How many head do you have here?" she asked, lifting her chin in the direction of the cows.

"This is just part of the herd. We have moved some of them up to spring range already. However, this is the second half and there's about five hundred head. We've been pushing them into this pasture now for the last couple weeks and they've eaten it down pretty far."

She looked around and, sure enough, the grass had been munched down to nubs and there were distinct mud trails all around the edges of the pasture that she could see.

Emily didn't know much about how open range worked, but she knew that in the State of Montana it was legal for ranchers to put their cattle on public lands during the summer months. It was part of agreements made during pioneering days, and it was still in effect. The law helped families keep large herds of cattle, and the animals' grazing helped decrease fire danger in national forests.

Not everyone liked it, but it had been a mutually beneficial relationship for the state and cattle growers for decades. It also helped keep public lands out of the hands of private buyers.

For those reasons, she would always be a fan.

"We need to find the lead heifer and get her moving. After we do, most of the others will follow her." He pointed in the direction of the mountains. "We're going to run them east and up that drainage there." He motioned toward a ravine that gradually moved up between the two mountains nearest them.

"Are all these heifers?" She didn't know anything about

cows other than brown cows did not, in fact, produce chocolate milk, like her ranching grandfather had once tried to convince her. She chuckled at the memory.

"No, we have some steers that we cut this spring in the group. They'll go to sale in the fall, but we need to fatten them up first period. That's another reason that the range is so important."

"Where is Trevor? Do you have any idea?" She looked at the ravine in the mountains where they were riding up to, searching for roads, but men were obvious.

"There's a good chance we'll catch him on the dirt road that runs along the base of the mountain there—you can't really see it because of the timber. It's an old logging road, and it's pretty beat up. Locals use it for summer recreation, us ranchers use it for the cattle and then hunters use it in the fall, but that's about it." He paused. "Actually, that's not entirely true. Now that there's all these new mapping apps, which show all the roads, we've had a lot more traffic. It's not a secret anymore."

She nodded, not sure what to say. Technology was a double-edged sword.

They rode in silence for a bit as she thought about how much Stacy would have loved to have been along. She'd always loved horses. She had a collection of them in her bedroom. Maybe one of these days Emily could bring her out to the ranch and introduce her to Ginger or one of the other gentle horses that they had in the stables.

She thought about Stacy pretending there were cowboys with her little horses and how there had been cattle rustlers stealing away her best black stallion while she played. It had been up to the cowboys to bring back the stallion, it had been a whole *thing*.

"Does anyone ever bother your cattle when they're on the range?"

"We always lose one or two. A lot of times it's to grizzly bears or wolves. We're pretty close to Glacier Park, and as a result there's lots of predation. As for people, you know as well as I do it's hard to predict what they will do. So far, we've been lucky, but we have found strange things up here over the years. One year we even found a deserted truck that someone had stolen and abandoned in the woods."

"This would be a good place for something like that," she said, brushing her hair out of her face.

"What's that?" he asked.

"Making something disappear, or someone."

He studied her for a minute with an impish grin on his face. "Do I have to worry about you making *me* disappear? That sounded a little evil." He laughed.

"That's not how I meant it at all, and you know that."

He shrugged playfully. "You know anybody could be the killer. Who's to say you weren't dating my brother and you ran afoul of him or something? *Duh duh duh...*" he hummed, like the thrumming of a murder mystery game show hook.

She was glad he could joke around about his loss; it showed he was starting to heal. She pointed to his cowboy hat. "Just like you white-hat wearers, I'm one of the good guys."

They weaved their horses through the cattle until he seemed to spot what appeared to be the lead cow and he picked his way over toward her. "Was it the hat that gave me away? That's how you decided that I was a good guy?" He chuckled. "If it's that simple to convince the cops, I'm surprised all criminals don't just adopt white hats." He tipped the brim in her direction.

"Well, now I don't know what to think, if you're acting all cute with me like that. Maybe you're trying too hard." She sent him a wide, playful smile.

He slapped her gently with the extra length of reins in his hand. "I don't have to be so nice," he said, a sultry edge in his voice that made her think of last night's activities.

Emily couldn't wait for another chance to be in his arms. With Stacy coming home, they may not get another opportunity. It pulled at her heart. They would have to take things slow from here, one day at a time. It would all depend on how things went when Stacy got back.

She knew her role as a mother was the crux of her identity. She couldn't help it, it was who she was—and would always be. Her daughter was the most important thing in her life and would continue to be, even when she grew up and moved away. Any man in her life would have to understand that and be on board—and in support of them both. That was something she hadn't really talked about with Cameron.

He slipped a leather strap loose on his saddle and took hold of his rope, or lariat, as he had called it when they had been getting the horses saddled up to go out. "That's our girl, right there," he said, pointing at the one he had seemed to take notice of as the lead cow. "I'm going to rope her and then get her moving with me. Sometimes that's a little easier, as long as she doesn't throw a fit. If she does, we may have a bit of a rodeo on our hands."

She nibbled on her lip, envisioning herself on the back of a bucking bronco. "If things do go sideways, what do you want me to do?"

"Ginger is a good girl, just lead her away. You're in control."

Emily tried to calm her racing heart by taking a slow,

deep breath but it wasn't as effective as she had hoped. Ginger tilted her ear back like she was a schoolteacher pointing at her in reprimand. She sat up straighter in the saddle and steeled her resolve. She had to trust Ginger.

Cameron swirled the lariat over his head, extending the rope as it revolved and then he loosed it. It arched over the cow's head and he pulled it back and wrapped it around the saddle's horn. The heifer jerked with surprise but didn't fight the lead. Instead, she looked lazily back at Cameron, the whites of her eyes showing as she chewed her cud.

Cameron huffed a laugh.

"Are you kidding me?" Emily asked, almost disappointed by the lack of excitement and the cow's response. "I thought there were going to be fireworks. You just wanted to show off your rope work, didn't you?"

He sent her that sexy smile. "You didn't think I was really gonna put you in danger, did you?"

She tried to slap him with the loose ends of her reins this time, but she missed him by a mile. He laughed at her.

"You have a long way to go before you're gonna be a full-on cowgirl, but I'll get you there."

"Is that right?" she teased. "Do you think I'm gonna be sticking around long enough for you to train me?" She tried to stop the excitement and giddiness she felt from entering her voice. All she wanted to do was become his cowgirl.

"If you're not interested…"

She shrugged. "I don't know if I'm interested in dating a showoff." She motioned to the lariat in his hand.

He rode up to the black cow and slipped the loop off her neck and scratched behind her ear. The yellow number tag on her ear read 82. "Eighty-two here has been around for a long time, at least for cow standards. She's been the lead for the last couple drives. She's my buddy." He tapped her on the haunches and she started plodding forward. "She'll pretty much follow us wherever we go. Then the other ones will line up. You just have to ride next to me."

"If it's this easy, do we even need Trevor and the other hands at all?" She glanced up at the mountain draw in front of them. It wasn't that far, maybe another half mile and they'd be to the mouth of the ravine.

"First, they're animals. Everything can change in a split second. Cows are not known for their intelligence, either. A single bee can throw this all off."

She nodded. She had seen enough movies to understand a stampede.

"Plus, normally it's the calves that you have to watch for. They tend to get split up from their mothers and start bawling. Then the mothers straggle behind trying to get to their little ones and it causes problems. So, you need a couple guys behind to pick up the loose head."

"If you want, I can ride in the back of the herd and help there until they arrive."

His face scrunched like he was seriously considering her offer but was torn. She was glad to see him look like that because she didn't want to leave him. "Let's just keep you up here for now. I don't want you getting hurt. If something happened back there, I wouldn't know, and I couldn't help you quickly enough."

Just when she thought she couldn't like him more. There he went, making her fall for him again. He was such a gentleman.

"When we get on the other side of this fence, though, and we get into the open range, I might have to change things up if Trevor's not up there. When the cows start breaking loose and wandering, I may need you to work that back end a little bit more and push them forward. I don't want them trying to get back in the pasture."

It made sense, but she silently begged that Trevor would be there.

"We also can't let them start going up or down that logging road. They just have to go straight across and up the drainage. Sometimes that's where they get a little confused. I like to set a cowboy on each side of the herd to push them up there, so they don't get any stupid ideas."

"Well, here's hoping Trevor and your other hands are there." The last thing she wanted was to have to chase down stray cows. She doubted the rest of them would be as amenable to her roping them or leading them as 82 was with Cameron.

She glanced behind them and 82 was still plodding along, its hoofs clomping in the dirt and kicking up mud as she moved directly in line behind his horse. The rest of the cattle had started to do exactly what Cameron had told her they would, and they were lining up behind the lead cow in single file.

She wondered what they thought. Either they thought they were going to be fed, they were incredibly trusting, or, as Cameron had said, kind of lacking intelligence.

Then again, lining up was not a sign of stupidity, it was just a sign of conformity. And one could argue that it could be used as a way to escape predation. However, she had a feeling that she was giving them way too much credit.

As they neared the edge of the pasture leading to the logging road and the mouth of the draw, Emily had to re-adjust her bellyband slightly. The end of the mag and the grip on the Glock had started to rub against her chest and take off a thin layer of skin.

This was the first time she'd had that problem, but it

was the bellyband or the saddle sore on her behind. In this case, it was a lot easier to adjust the band and loosen her gun. She dropped it down, letting the gun sit just over her belt buckle with the band barely folded.

She'd have to remember to readjust it before getting down or it would flop off if she wasn't careful.

"I think I see the ranch truck," Cameron said, pointing ahead.

She was relieved. They'd have this handled in no time. Then they could go back to trying to get answers for Bullock. She checked her phone one more time, hoping to see an e-mail pop up with information about their unknown suspect, but there was nothing on the subject. The only e-mails she'd received were the standards in office garbage and one from the medical examiner's office that Bullock had forwarded.

She clicked on that e-mail and opened the attachment, which included the autopsy report for Ben. She scanned the findings; most were what they had expected. Cameron's brother had died from a gunshot wound, consistent with that of a 9mm handgun. They had found part of the bullet lodged within his skull.

From the bullet and the gun that was recovered on scene, they were able to say conclusively that the round that killed him had come from the gun found in his hand. However, due to the angle of entry and exit, it could not have been Ben who had fired the weapon.

Again, it didn't come as a surprise.

According to the examiner, they were placing the time of death at approximately 5:00 a.m.

She closed the report and clicked on the second attachment, which was for Leonard. Again, there weren't many surprises. He had suffered from a series of ante-mortem stab wounds, consistent with that inflicted by a 7-inch blade at or near the time of death. However, the wound that had likely killed him was a stab wound to the aorta. That wound had caused the man to bleed out almost instantly.

According to the examiner, they had put his time of death at approximately 4:00 a.m.

She stared at her phone. This meant conclusively that Leonard could not have killed Ben. There was no way. And whoever had killed Leonard, had likely murdered Ben as well.

With the e-mails was a simple note that read, *Thought you might find this interesting.*

That was an understatement.

As they rode up to the edge of the pasture, they approached a ranch pickup that looked similar to the one where she had found Leonard's body. Seeing that pickup, she had a sinking feeling that once again she was going to have to deal with a whole lot more than she'd bargained for—and this time, she may well be walking into a killer's trap.

Chapter Nineteen

Cameron didn't see Trevor or one of the hands he'd brought along anywhere. In fact, there weren't even horses tied to the trailer, as he would have expected. He stopped, trying to listen for the sounds of footfalls within the metal trailer. By now, if the horses were inside, they would be getting antsy, especially with the noise of the cows so close by. However, he heard nothing.

"Why don't you wait here for a second? I'm gonna go check on things. I'll be right back. Keep an eye on 82." He motioned toward the lead.

Emily nodded.

He knew she had no clue what to do if that old cow wandered off, but he could get things back under control if she failed. He just needed to give Emily a task to keep her mind occupied, so she didn't worry. She was able to read his face and know what he was thinking, and it didn't always work out to his advantage.

For some reason, things with Trevor weren't feeling quite right lately, and he didn't know why. He trusted Trevor and he always had. It was unlike him to not be around when Cam needed him the most.

Yet, his absence could have meant many things—the most glaring being that he was somehow complicit. That was something that didn't sit well with Cameron as, in most ways, Leonard was as much the ranch hand's dad as he was Cameron's. For Trevor to kill him would have been tantamount to patricide.

The only conceivable way he could think of Trevor doing something to hurt his dad would be if he'd done it accidentally or drunkenly, but he couldn't imagine that Trevor wouldn't turn himself in. He loved this family. At the bare minimum, he would have told Cam then run off or something.

There's no way Trevor could have been behind the murders. He was just off center right now.

Then again, he was even off the mark with the cattle, which was unheard of. He was never this disorganized when moving herds, and Cameron didn't like it.

He opened the gate, and he and Bessie slipped through and he closed it behind him, making sure the cow didn't follow. He rode up to the horse trailer and peeked inside, but it was empty. It didn't even appear as if there had been horses inside it all.

That was strange. Trevor had to have brought the horses here somehow. There hadn't been any sign of them on the ride up from the barn.

He tried not to panic.

Trevor wouldn't drive a truck up here with a trailer without horses in it. He knew the work that needed to be done. He wouldn't waste the gas. This made no sense.

He reached down and patted his pocket. All he was carrying with him was his standard pocketknife and a black bandanna. He glanced over at Emily. From where he was sitting, he could tell she was carrying a gun.

It had been stupid of him not to bring a handgun on their little drive, but he normally didn't—in the many years they had been moving their cattle up the mountain, he'd never needed one. His dad was always the one who brought a pistol. It was just their system. Rarely had they ever needed one. In fact, he believed in bear spray when it came to predators on their cows, which had never been a problem during a drive.

Most of the time, carrying a gun on the hip was more uncomfortable than it was worth, and it was why he didn't do it. But he definitely regretted the decision today.

He tried to tell himself that he was making something out of nothing.

Maybe Trevor had just parked the empty trailer here and was riding in from somewhere else. Or maybe the other ranch hand had driven the trailer here and walked or gotten a ride back. There were a lot of scenarios that Cam could be missing. He took his phone out and sent a quick message to Trevor.

He waited a long moment, but in true Trevor fashion, the message remained unread.

If everything proved to be in his head, Cameron and his pseudo brother were going to have a serious conversation as soon as they got back to the ranch house. This not answering the phone thing was driving him crazy. It was like having a kid around.

He thought of Stacy—a five-year-old had to be easier to deal with. In her case, at least Emily didn't expect her to answer the phone.

Hopefully, Stacy was safe and would be home soon.

As much as Cam wanted to pummel Todd, he would have to be careful about which battles he could fight. Emily had a lot to lose when it came to her daughter, and he couldn't make things worse by acting a fool.

If they were going to become a major part of his life,

as he hoped, Todd wasn't the only man who needed to respect boundaries.

He looked around the truck, but there weren't any prints he could see, and everything seemed in order. He tried to tell himself that the knot in his gut was just an overreaction and he was being hypervigilant for no reason.

Trevor had probably just parked the truck there, empty for later, and jumped in another rig to go get the horses and then leave from the barn. They were probably behind them and looking for the cattle. No big deal.

If Trevor and no other hands were there, he and Emily were just going to have to do this themselves. He didn't want to wait all day and risk having the cows mill around again in the pasture for no reason.

Tag 82 had been pretty amenable. All they had to do was get her up the draw another half mile. It wouldn't be a problem. Emily had been doing great on the horse.

He waved his fingers at Emily, getting her attention. "Why don't you go ahead and open the gate and lead that cow through? Let's just start moving them up. If they're pushing the cows from behind, we don't want them bunching up. That will create problems and we don't want them getting into the barbed wire."

She nodded. "You got it."

"First," he said, putting his finger up, "I'm going to move the ranch truck sideways on the road, it can act as a barrier for the cows. That will keep them moving forward. Then we only have to worry about the one side."

She gave him the thumbs-up, turned the horse around and moved some of the cows back from the fence. Though she had said she didn't know much about horses, it was clear that her time on her grandparent's ranch had stuck with her. It was funny how sometimes the work done as a kid had a way of imprinting on a person and almost becoming muscle memory.

He rode over to a big pine on the far side of the road and tied up Bessie, who gave him the stink eye as he climbed down.

"Don't worry, I'm not leaving you here."

It might have been in his head, but he could have sworn that the normally sassy horse was not herself since his father's passing. She hadn't even tried to buck him or ignore his lead today. That was totally unlike the paint. He felt for her. Before he walked away, he gave her a good scratch and she closed her eyes in gratitude.

When he was done, he walked over to the truck and opened the unlocked door. Like all the ranch trucks, he flipped down the visor and the keys fell into his hand. The system was one that saved everyone steps and headaches as it wasn't uncommon for a person to have to move vehicles around or run a truck from one place to another in a hurry. No one needed to ask to use one; as far as they were concerned, it was just another tool.

Thrown in the passenger seat was a white sweatshirt with an embroidered red Canadian maple leaf on the front. From the tag, it was a woman's size small. There was what looked like blood on the wrists and up the arms. He stared at it for a long moment.

There wasn't a woman working on the ranch.

Trevor didn't have a girlfriend.

As of right now, Trevor *was missing*.

How would a woman have known to bring the truck out here and why would she have?

He moved to back up and close the driver's-side door. As he backed up, he felt a cold steel barrel press against the base of his skull. "Don't move, or I will put a bullet in you just like I did your brother," a man said.

He didn't recognize the voice.

He looked up through the front glass of the pickup to see if Emily was watching, but she had her back to him and was working with the cows behind the fence in the pasture. She had no idea anything was happening.

He thought about calling out to her, but even if she heard him, it wouldn't do any good and it would only put them in further danger.

Where had the man come from?

"What do you want?" he asked, trying his best to remain calm. He wanted to turn around and face the man, but he was afraid to move. This dude, whoever he was, wasn't afraid to kill—he'd already proven that.

If Cameron was to survive and keep Emily from getting hurt, he was going to have to play along. First things first, he needed to make sure Emily didn't find herself in the line of fire.

"I want you to know, none of this had to happen." The man sounded torn, almost apologetic.

Cam took it as a good sign. At least the guy holding the gun to his head wasn't just some psychotic killer who would just kill anyone without reason and without feeling some sense of remorse. That was something he could perhaps work with to keep things under control—and this man's sense of remorse could perhaps even keep Cam alive.

"Why is that, man?" he asked, trying to sound empathetic.

The gun shook violently, like the man's hand was getting tired, or else he was starting to lose his nerve.

"Because…your brother shouldn't have been such an idiot. I told him not to come here. I told him."

Cameron turned around. Standing there with that self-righteous smirk he'd seen once before, was Todd. However, standing not ten feet behind him and looking beaten down, was Trevor.

"Todd? Trevor?" He was so confused. He didn't have a clue these guys even knew each other. "Todd, I thought you were in Canada?"

"I needed an alibi in case I had to murder you." He shrugged.

His stomach clenched. "How did you know my brother?"

Todd lowered the gun, but kept it pressed into Cam's stomach, not letting him forget that it was there if he tried something stupid.

"Your brother and I had a good thing going with your father and the ranch." He nudged his chin in the direction of Emily and the pasture. "If you don't do anything stupid, maybe we can keep that good thing going."

Cam had no idea what Todd was talking about, but whatever his father, Ben and Trevor had found themselves a part of…clearly, he didn't want to be involved, even if Todd hadn't been the ringleader. Having Todd at the helm only made it that much easier to tell him to pound sand.

However, Cam had to wait.

"I'm listening," he said, the gun digging into his shirt.

"First," Todd said, looking over at Emily, "you need to get that witch Emily over here and put her in the trailer. She needs to be out of our way."

He wasn't going for that idea. He wasn't locking her anywhere. "No."

"If you don't put her in the trailer, cool, calm and collected like—without setting off the alarms—then I will just go ahead and shoot her. If I did, it would solve a hell of a lot of problems for me." Todd sucked his teeth. "The only reason I ain't already is that my daughter loves her mama."

So, the guy did have some kind of heart—even if it was fetid and black.

Trevor finally walked over. "I'm sorry, Cam. I didn't want none of this to happen. I told your dad just to go with everything your brother wanted, but he didn't want things your brother's way. He said he wanted out. They got into a fight."

"He wanted out of *what*?"

Trevor looked at his boots. "They were running girls out of Canada—Fernie—through here sometimes and then into North Dakota and into the rough-necking camps. Your dad was laundering the money for your brother."

"What in the—" His father had done a lot of things to make ends meet at the ranch, but making money like that was something he'd never thought Leonard'd stoop to.

"He didn't know what Ben was doin'," Trevor continued. "He was just taking his cut. Yet when your brother stopped by this time, he had one of the girls with him. Your dad figured it out. He blew a rod and Ben had to take him out."

Cameron hated what his father had done in laundering the money. Who knows what would happen with the ranch if Detective Bullock found out, but at least he'd put his foot down with the rest. His father had tried to do the right thing in the end; it had cost him his life.

And his son had been the one to kill him. The truth slashed at Cam like grizzly claws.

"Your brother was doing a lot of drugs," Todd said. "He had become a liability. I'm sure you will see that in the paperwork you get back eventually. It's why I had my girl kill him. She knew it was either him or her who had to die to appease me. They weren't supposed to kill Leonard. They screwed everything up."

Trevor motioned toward Emily. "I'll go get her. She knows me."

Todd nodded. "Be quick about it."

"Don't hurt her and don't you dare put her in that trailer," Cam said to Trevor.

Trevor nodded.

He trusted Trevor a whole lot more than he trusted Todd, but it was his blind trust of Trevor that had led him to this moment. Trevor had known all along who had been involved in the murders and he had lied.

"Trevor, why *did* you lie to me about this? If you knew what had happened at the ranch, why didn't you at least give me a heads-up, so I didn't think someone also wanted me dead?"

"Who said I don't?" Todd asked.

"If you did, I would already be piled up on the ground." He pointed at the dirt beside the pickup.

"I was going to, but you haven't been without that woman. I was gonna tell you at the bar, but all you were doing was making eyes at her. I figured you'd just go and tell her what we'd done and I'd have my ass in jail." Trevor sighed. "I just needed a chance to get you to understand."

"After all my father and I have done for you, why would you go against him?"

Trevor shook his head adamantly. "I wasn't, I swear. I was trying to make him see that he needed to keep doing business with Todd and Ben. They were keeping the ranch afloat. I was on the ranch's side."

Todd pointed at Trevor like his statement was a testimonial.

"Maybe you can listen to me better than your father," Trevor continued. "All I want, is to run sixty thousand dollars more a month."

He thought back to the banking records. "So, you want one-hundred-thousand dollars a month through us? That will draw some red flags. And how can we make that look legitimate in the ranching industry? We don't work with that kind of cash."

"No, but marijuana is legal in the State of Montana, and it is a cash-based industry," Todd said. "Put up some greenhouses. I don't care if you don't grow anything. Just do the paperwork."

"Where will I get the money for all this *paperwork*?" he asked, playing along.

"I'll give you one-hundred-thousand dollars in cash this week to start. All you have to do is say yes. From then on, you will take care of our money. You can take ten percent. Same as your father."

"Twenty and I have conditions."

"Fifteen and what are these conditions?" Todd countered.

"First, return Stacy, leave Emily out of this and give her full custody—no more renegotiation or mediation. Second, I want the girl who killed my brother. She needs to pay. There has to be justice."

Todd stared at him for a solid minute and there was a smirk on his lips. "You don't know what you are asking."

Oh, but he did. He was putting a price on Todd's child and forcing this man to stop using his daughter as a pawn. Stacy deserved better.

He pushed Todd off him. "Bring me the woman and

bring Emily the signed parenting agreement tomorrow. If you do, I'll do as you want. Okay?"

Todd sent him a devilish, fanged grin. "You have a deal."

Chapter Twenty

Cameron came riding up beside her on Bessie, his face was ashen and gaunt like he had been sick.

"Are you okay?" Emily asked, wanting to reach over and check his temperature with her hand, but he was too far away.

He nodded, but he didn't say anything. "Let's go." He motioned back toward the ranch.

"What?" she asked, confused. "Don't we need to move the cows into the summer range?"

He was riding ahead of her back in the direction in which they had come. The cows they'd led up and that she'd been trying to keep from wandering off were now starting to scatter every which way. It didn't make sense. None of it.

They'd been having fun, they'd been going to drive the cows across the road, he'd gone to the truck and now this.

He must be sick.

She tried not to be worried.

Even sick, she would have thought he would have made sure the cows had been moved up that draw. They were so close to getting it done. All they had to do was move them another half mile. The majority of the work had already been done.

Plus, he'd just left the truck sitting there—abandoned. Why? What had been inside?

Nothing made sense.

Her cop alarm bells were going off like mad.

"Cam?" she called after him, but he didn't even look back at her and he kept riding. "Cameron?" she called again. Again, he didn't slow down.

She nudged her horse into a trot as they broke through the tail end of the herd of cows.

Ginger's hooves thumped on the dirt and she moved faster, but as she did, so did Bessie and Cameron in front of them.

He didn't want her to catch him.

What in the...

The wind whistled by her ears as they picked up speed and she stood in the stirrups. She leaned forward slightly and let her knees take the impact of the horse's footfalls. Her hair broke free of her hair tie with the jarring force of the wind and the gallop and she couldn't help the laugh that tore from her lips. The sound was half crazed and free, but it felt as good as the wind on her face and the whirring speed of the horse beneath her. In this wild moment, she was the predator in a chase and damn if it didn't feel great.

The bay struggled, but she finally reached the paint. Emily had a feeling that Cameron had pulled up and allowed them to catch up as Ginger had more speed than most horses she had seen that weren't thoroughbreds. It was as if that horse had come straight off the wild herds of the plains from generations past. She was a thing of beauty.

The ranch house was in sight as they slowed down. It was amazing how fast the trip back was compared to their slow plod with the cows up had been.

"Are you going to tell me what's wrong or are you going

to make me actually take you into the interview room at the station this time?" she teased, hoping that it would make him laugh and open up.

Instead, the smile that had formed on his lips from the ride vanished and his eyes widened. Some of the color in his cheeks disappeared. "Everything is fine. I think that it's best if you head back to your place though. You need to get things handled with your daughter."

Your daughter? The way he'd said that was so cold and clinical. It was as if he was a stranger.

Emily and Stacy hadn't known Cameron that long. Yet so much had happened. So much had changed and developed in such a short amount of time that it felt like the world had flipped and he was now at the center of hers.

She didn't know how to respond or what to think.

She was just *hurt*.

"Just head back to the barn and tie Ginger up at the post there." He motioned to the hitching post out front. "I'll unsaddle her. You just go."

Just like that, she was dismissed.

CAMERON WALKED INTO the barn and started unsaddling Ginger. He slipped off the reins and put on her halter and tied her to the loop in the barn so he could take care of her while Bessie waited outside.

He was a disaster. He didn't know what to do and now he could tell that he had hurt the one person he loved. In fact, she was the only person he had left in this world whom he cared about—well, except her daughter, but they were really a package deal.

He smiled at the thought.

If nothing else, if he just went along with the stupid deal like he'd promised, he could check a lot of boxes. He could save the ranch, save Emily and her daughter, and never have to worry about the financial future of the place again. Plus, he'd solved the murder and there would be some sort of justice for his brother's death.

Or, at least there could be—but what would he do with the woman once Todd brought her to him?

He wasn't a judge.

Just because Todd told him that the murder had happened that way didn't mean it had. People lied all the time and Todd was definitely not above it—even if the bloody sweatshirt and the handprints seemed to back up his account.

He pulled the saddle off Ginger's back along with the blanket. It was wet with sweat, and he carried it over to the tack room and hung it on the rack. He grabbed a currycomb and headed back to the waiting horse. She leaned into him as he started to rub her down.

If he just turned this all over to Bullock, then the detective could be the one to start the wheels of justice. Yet, if Cameron told Bullock, he put the future of the ranch at risk and would put the legacy of his family in jeopardy.

He couldn't be the one to lose everything…even if it was his father's choices that had gotten them to this point, Cam was the one who was risking his future.

There had to be a way to get ahead of this and handle it in a manner that he could get everything he wanted, but he didn't live in some fantasy world. This was his reality and reality didn't work that way. He couldn't get everything he wanted, no one ever did.

It felt like it came down to a singular, heartbreaking choice—love or legacy.

He'd only known Emily and her daughter for a few days, but it was all it had taken to know they were what he wanted in his ideal world. Yet the ranch had been his entire life up to this point, and it had consumed the lives of multiple generations before him.

If he became a criminal, he could save it all and maybe even get the girl—that was, if she would want to be with a morally gray man.

There was no way.

He loved Emily and he respected the sacrifices of his family, but he would never allow himself to follow the path his brother had taken and condone human trafficking. It sickened him.

He'd loved his brother as a child, but he hated the man he'd become after he'd left the ranch. That was to say nothing of the effects he had upon Cam when he'd had the affair with April.

He just couldn't understand how his brother had so dramatically lost his way.

Todd had said he'd been using drugs. It fell in line with his devolving behavior and morals, but it also made Cam feel as if he had failed his brother by not seeing the signs and getting him help earlier.

He had failed in so many ways, but none of that mattered now. All that mattered was that he made the right choices moving forward.

He had twenty-four hours before meeting Todd and Trevor to figure out exactly what those right choices were and what they meant for his future.

Chapter Twenty-One

Emily had been a cop long enough to trust her gut. When something, or someone, felt *off*, she acted, and she didn't question herself. It was one of the things in this job that gave her a leg up on the rest of the world. And, man oh man, was Cameron *off*.

As soon as she'd arrived at the ranch, she'd gotten into her car and, instead of heading home or back to town, had turned down the road that veered off the ranch road and headed back up toward where the ranch truck and trailer had been parked.

The logging road wyed and she took the right fork, but even though it was the logically correct direction, it wasn't how logging roads always worked. Sometimes they double-backed, went straight up or came to an abrupt dead end. So, instead of driving aimlessly in hopes she was going the right way, she pulled over to check the maps to make sure she was on the right road.

Of course, her service was cutting out and the internet was painfully slow. Sometimes it was just the car that caused the problem.

Getting out, she walked back a little bit toward the wye to get better service. As she did, she heard the distinct sound of a truck coming toward her. Not wanting to be noticed, she stepped into the timber and brush that lined the roadside. She hunkered down, concealing herself as best she could while holding on to an azalea bush that provided ground cover beside her.

Unless someone was really paying attention, she was sure she wouldn't be seen.

Coming around the corner and kicking up dust was the red Ford she knew only too well. Todd was in the driver's seat and Trevor was riding next to him. It was hard to tell from where she sat, but it looked like there were other people in the back seat of the pickup as well.

She gasped as she gripped the bush harder, letting the little branches pierce the soft flesh of her palm.

Why were Todd and Trevor together?

It dawned on her.

They had to have been working together. That meant only one thing—Todd was somehow connected to what was happening on the ranch.

She didn't understand how or why, but she wasn't surprised. That was why Todd had dumped Stacy on her in the middle of her investigation. He'd done that on purpose to make things more complicated. He had wanted to slow them down, or at least keep her out of it.

Of course, she was the one who could most easily recognize him if given the opportunity.

No wonder Cam had been acting so strange.

He had told her to go home, to wait for Stacy.

Had he made some kind of bargain?

He would.

There was no doubt in her mind that he would do anything to keep Stacy, and her, safe. That also meant putting himself in danger.

She couldn't let him risk himself for them.

The Ford went racing by. In the back was a woman she didn't recognize and, beside her, with her thumb in her mouth, was Stacy.

Her heart plummeted.

She needed her daughter back.

She needed Stacy tucked safely in her arms and away from that man.

As soon as they were out of view, she raced to her car. Before getting in, she called Detective Bullock. He answered on the first ring. "I think I have our killers," she said, sounding breathless. "They are in a red Ford F-150 driven by Todd Monahan."

"Your ex-husband?" Bullock asked, shock rattling his voice.

"Yes."

"I know. Your friend Cameron already called and told me what happened."

She paused, surprised that Cam had decided to call Bullock but not her—he must have had his reasons. She didn't know everything that had happened, but she could find out Cameron's reasons for everything later. Right now, she needed to worry about her daughter. "Stacy is in that pickup along with two other occupants, Trevor and an unknown woman. They are headed in the direction of the WGC Ranch."

"I have everyone headed in that direction. Don't do anything until you have backup," Bullock ordered. "I need you to become the next detective in my unit, and I don't need you getting hurt."

If he'd said that in any other moment, she would have smiled and been excited, but right now she barely heard him. "Thanks, boss. I'll try to hold."

"Don't try. Do."

She hung up the phone and climbed into her patrol car. She needed to get to Stacy.

Until now, she had hated Todd and thought he was a nuisance, but she'd never thought he was a real threat to her daughter's safety. She should have known better. A man who could basically kidnap his child and take her across international borders without consent didn't have compassion for others, or many moral boundaries.

She'd had a child with a monster.

Her monster had become Cameron's monster, too.

Emily sucked in a choking cry. She didn't have time to feel right now. There was only time for action and to set things right. There was only time to save her daughter and seek justice.

No matter what Bullock said, she couldn't wait to get her daughter back. She needed to know she was safe.

She started her engine and hit the gas. She drove as fast as she could, fishtailing in the light car on the corners. She didn't care as she hit the accelerator coming out of the curves.

Todd must have been going fifty and he'd had one heck of a head start.

It wasn't until she was on the straightaway and out of the timbered area that she spotted Todd's pickup. He was almost to the driveway of the ranch.

She flipped on her lights and sirens and pushed the car to the max, coming up fast on him.

As she neared, she saw Stacy's little head pop up in the back window. She smiled and waved, but the brunette woman beside her grabbed her and pushed her down.

Anger pulsed through Emily. She didn't know who the woman was, but she had no right to touch her daughter.

The woman would pay.

Instead of slowing down and pulling over, Todd sped up. She couldn't believe it. There was no way her ex was going to put her daughter in even further danger by getting in a high-speed chase with her.

Emily turned on the loudspeaker. "Todd Monahan, pull over. I repeat, pull the vehicle over!"

She let Dispatch know she was in pursuit. Bullock was going to be furious, but it was too late to stop now.

As the truck neared the entrance of the ranch, a black Ford pickup pulled out in front of him, blocking the road. There was a barbed-wire fence on both sides of the road. There was no going around. Todd only had one option—stop or T-bone the truck.

He skidded to a stop, but she knew it wasn't to keep their daughter safe—he just loved that truck too much to allow it to be damaged.

Cameron stepped out of his pickup and, raising a rifle to his shoulder, took aim squarely at Todd.

She went back to the loudspeaker. "Cameron, don't!" she screamed. She pressed the gas as hard as she could.

She drove as fast as she could, careening down the road and skidding to a sideways stop behind Todd's pickup and boxing him in.

"No one shoot!" she yelled over the loudspeaker.

If anyone fired a weapon, Stacy would be caught in the crossfire.

She threw her gear into Park and drew the Glock from her bellyband as she got out of the car. She pointed it straight at the driver's-side door.

"Todd, put your hands out of the window!" she ordered.

Todd opened the door of his pickup, not following instructions.

"Don't take another step or I will be forced to shoot!" she yelled.

Todd stepped out of the truck and turned to face her. His right hand was on the door of the pickup, but his other was still inside the truck. She couldn't tell what he was holding.

She didn't want to shoot.

If he was holding a gun, it could take him less than a second to draw and shoot. He could kill her in a second.

Her daughter could be a witness to her murder.

Or Stacy could be a witness to her shooting her father in self-defense.

She didn't want her to see any of this.

Her gaze flickered to the back window. Stacy's little face was staring out at her.

As she glanced back at Todd, his hand had moved. It was behind his back.

"Get on the ground, Todd!" She felt almost manic.

Everything she had learned at the academy told her to shoot. She was well within her rights, but if there was nothing in his hand or if it was just a cell phone or something, she would come out of this event looking like an overzealous cop—or worse, a vengeful ex-wife. Every part of this investigation would be analyzed after the fact. She was going to be heavily scrutinized. She had to be so careful.

Yet her life and her daughter's welfare were on the line.

Cameron stepped around the front of Todd's truck to the right. "Trevor, April, get out!" he yelled, motioning toward them with his rifle.

April? The woman in the truck—the one who'd had the nerve to touch her daughter—was his ex-wife?

Oh, she was so going to jail.

Trevor opened the door and climbed out. He dropped

to the ground and laid down with his hands on the back of his head. At least he had a brain.

The woman followed suit.

Todd, however, kept walking toward her.

"Put your hands above your head, Todd. If you don't, I will be forced to shoot!" she ordered.

Todd moved his hands slowly to where she could see them. In the hand, which had been behind his back, was a cell phone.

She rushed toward him and shoulder-checked him, throwing him to the ground. As she moved, he reached for her gun. He caught her off guard and, in his fight, took hold of her gun. She tried to twist it free of his hand, but he was so strong.

She wrestled for it, trying to get it back. With her right hand, she reached down and unholstered her other weapon. Pushing it up into his ribs, she pulled the trigger. She would never forget the sound or the feel of the gases exploding from the end of the barrel between their wrestling bodies.

Todd made a gurgling sound and his body went limp. She'd never wanted to be drawn into in an officer-involved shooting—but Todd had made the choice. He had never respected her, and in this case, he'd forgotten who she was at her core—a warrior.

Chapter Twenty-Two

Stacy was sitting on Cam's shoulders as they walked out into the center of the pasture. She was giggling as Cameron pretended to be a pony, trotting around and making her bounce.

The sight made Emily smile.

They had been through so much in the last couple of months that it was a relief to just relax and enjoy the last lazy days of summer.

Stacy had recovered remarkably well after learning about her father's death. Thankfully, she hadn't been able to see the fight or the shooting.

April was in jail awaiting sentencing after being found guilty of first-degree murder in the death of Benjamin Trapper. During the court testimonies, it had come out that she had continued her relationship with Ben and they had been working together to set up the trafficking ring. She was working as what they called a "bottom" or "right hand" and grooming women to feel safe to work under Ben and the guys running them in various areas of the country.

All in all, they had ended up identifying more than fifty women who'd been working for Ben and April, including the woman they had seen at the Arrow Lodge who had ripped the business card in two. She hadn't been happy to see them and, after the trial, she had disappeared once again.

They'd connected many of the women up with the resources, health care and counseling services they'd needed. Because of his help, Cameron and the ranch's corporation were given immunity for his father's roles in money laundering.

Todd's truck was sitting in the impound yard and would be going to the salvage yard to be recycled.

Emily couldn't be happier to know that his prized possession would soon be crushed.

"Mama, you coming?" Stacy asked, looking back at her. "Ginger is waiting!"

Emily hurried up, moving to their side. Cam reached down and took her hand with his.

Ginger, hearing her name from across the field, started to trot toward them. She was saddled up, which struck Emily as highly unusual.

They hadn't talked about taking Stacy riding today, but now Stacy's excitement made more sense.

Her daughter had fallen in love with Ginger the second she had set eyes on her, and the feeling had been mutual. What had once been Cameron's horse had instantly become Stacy's. He didn't have a hope of the bay mare ever being his again—and it was so much so, the horse's loyalties had even become a joke.

Ginger trotted to a gentle stop beside her girl. She lifted her head, waiting for the little girl's fingers to touch her nose. As she did, Ginger flipped her mane with excitement.

It was the sweetest thing.

"Let's get you up there in the saddle," Cam said, lifting Stacy off his shoulders and moving her into the saddle.

She giggled wildly, putting her hands over her mouth as she wiggled into the saddle. "Are you going to do it yet?"

He laughed. "*Shh…* Don't give it away."

She shook her head, clamping her hands over her mouth even harder and looking over at her mother and then back to Cam.

"What are you two up to?" Emily asked.

Stacy wiggled with excitement again, making Ginger look back at her with what amounted to a mare's smile.

"Do you want to get it out for her?" Cam asked.

Stacy reached into the panier behind the saddle and took out a little red-velvet box. "Can I show her?"

"Yes, ladybug," he said, using their now-shared nickname.

Emily's heart raced as she stared at the velvet box. That couldn't be what she hoped it was. She wiggled on her toes with excitement, like her daughter had in the saddle. She put her hands over her mouth as she giggled. "You aren't… You didn't!" she exclaimed, looking to Cam.

He smiled wildly. "I don't have to, if you are going to say no."

Stacy opened the box with far too much force and the ring inside jerked wildly. She and Cameron jumped to catch it just in case the ring inside went flying, and they bumped hard into one another.

"Oh…" Emily exclaimed. "That was close."

"To you saying no?" Cam teased.

"You haven't even asked." She smiled.

"True. May I have the ring?"

Stacy nodded.

Cameron took the box from Stacy and dropped to his knee as Stacy giggled. "Ms. Emily, I have loved you and Stacy from the first moment I met you. There is nothing I wouldn't do for you ladies." He smiled up at Emily. "Would you do me the honor of being my wife?"

Stacy squealed. "Mama, say yes!"

Emily laughed. "Should I?"

Stacy nodded wildly.

"Well, I got my marching orders." She smiled. "Yes, Cameron Trapper. I would love to be your wife."

Until she had met Cameron, Emily hadn't been a believer in true love. Yet, when she kissed him, she knew exactly what it meant—true love was knowing that through thick and thin, sickness and health, and peace and war, two people would stand with one another forever.

* * * * *